JOYCE'S PUPIL

Drago Jančar

Joyce's Pupil

A Brandon Original Paperback

First published in 2006 by Brandon
an imprint of Mount Eagle Publications
Dingle, Co. Kerry, Ireland, and
Unit 3, Olympia Trading Estate, Coburg Road, London N22 6TZ, England

ISBN 0 86322 340 0

2 4 6 8 10 9 7 5 3 1

Mount Eagle Publications receives support from
the Arts Council/An Chomhairle Ealaíon.

The publisher acknowledges the financial assistance of
Ireland Literature Exchange (Translation Fund), Dublin, Ireland.
www.irelandliterature.com
info@irelandliterature.com

Cover design: Anú Design
Typesetting by Red Barn Publishing, Skeagh, Skibbereen
Printed in the UK

CONTENTS

Joyce's Pupil

Another of Joyce's pupils was a young man of twenty named Boris Furlan...
Richard Ellman: *James Joyce*
(Oxford University Press, 1982), p. 341

1.

This story will end with a mob dragging an old man with a weak heart – a retired professor and former law school dean – out of his house and loading him on a wheelbarrow as they cry out in anger and derision. He will be pushed through the winding streets of the old town towards the river, to be dumped into its rushing, freezing current.

The final lines of the story will be cried out in Slovenian, in its upland, alpine dialect; mocking cries will resound on the street along which the wheelbarrow, with the

bouncing, helpless body on it, will rattle. A rain of impre-
cations, a beating shower of curses, a torrential flood of
laughter and a hail of furious abuse will fall upon the
professor's head, the inside of which will suddenly go completely blank, as if swallowed by a black hole.

2.

The first lines are spoken many years earlier, in English, in
the quiet of a Trieste apartment. It is evening. On the table
one can see a warm circle of light which radiates from a
beautifully fashioned oil lamp. The thirty-year-old English
teacher and his twenty-year-old pupil are bent over books and
papers. A strong north wind is blowing outside, searching for
a route through the streets to the sea. Shutters bang and the
sea foams against the shore; the swirling winds only accen-
tuate the tranquillity and safety of the room. The pupil reads
English sentences aloud, and the teacher patiently corrects
his pronunciation. When the lesson is over, the teacher walks
to the window and looks out on to the street where a piece
of paper blows and eddies in the wind. Perhaps he speaks in
his Irish accent about the language, perhaps about Thomas
Aquinas. After each lesson, pupil and teacher generally dis-
cuss philosophy. The pupil, like so many youths of the day,
is much taken with Schopenhauer and Nietzsche. The teacher
attempts to quell this enthusiasm; for him the only philoso-
pher is Aquinas, whose thought, in the teacher's opinion, is

8

as sharp as a sword blade. The teacher reads a page of his work in Latin every day.

The teacher sits back down and asks the pupil to describe the oil lamp in English. The pupil gets hopelessly tangled in technical expressions, and the teacher takes over from him, describing the oil lamp in exhaustive detail. He goes on for a full half hour, indulging a habit that many years later the student will call descriptive passion.

Professor Zois, the student cries out, I will never learn English. Professor Zois chuckles, in part out of satisfaction at his description, in part at the way the pupil mangles his name. That is how the Italians say it because they can't pronounce Joyce properly.

3.

After these conversations by the light of the oil lamp, Joyce's pupil, a young Slovenian law student from Trieste, suddenly felt a certain blankness in his head. A moment before he had been speaking freely with his teacher about Schopenhauer and Aquinas, about problems of morality and courage, but when he was confronted with the puzzle of the oil lamp, the fuel well, the glass chimney, the wick and all the rest of the parts that made up that insignificant object, he felt a gigantic hole opening up inside his head, a hole that swallowed up every thought, a kind of empty space in which nothing could be heard but the howl of the wind through the Trieste streets

9

on the way to the sea. The wind was growing stronger and beginning to roar to the sound of the voluptuously ornamented, albeit somewhat monotonous, speech of Professor Zois which emanated from the depths of his descriptive passion. And the gathering storm was also accompanied by the roars, howls and clamour of a gigantic crowd.

4.

Joyce and his Triestine student met for the last time on a hot July day in the summer of 1914. One could feel tension in the air throughout the city. Mobilised men were mustering near the barracks, while crowds shouting bellicose slogans milled on the streets and piazzas. The teacher, upset and worried, rapped on his young friend's apartment door. Then they looked through the windows of the pupil's room at the building of the Italian consulate, which was surrounded by an angry crowd. Encouraged by loud shouts, several of them tried to tear down the Italian flag. Stones were thrown at the façade; some panes of glass shattered; there was yelling. Joyce was clearly perturbed, and he worriedly asked his young friend what was going to happen. Professor Zois, he said with a laugh, there will be war. This scared his teacher. Joyce said that he would depart. When the shouts of the crowd grew louder he shut his eyes, then he turned around, and while his pupil was still speaking he ran out of the apartment and the building without saying a word. The pupil laughed; history was being made outside. He understood that some people can derive ineffable joy from describing an oil lamp, but he was interested in other things. The roar of the crowd heralded the arrival of momentous times. He was drawn outside, into the whirlwind.

5.

In the years that followed, the pupil developed into a determined and contented man. He succeeded at everything he started. His mind, which had been unable to comprehend his teacher's passion for description, inclined to analytic passions; Kant, Croce and Masaryk were stacked on his desk. He received his law degree from the University of Bologna. And he was attracted ever more strongly to the nervous agitation of European events, which whirled across the piazzas of Trieste like an Adriatic storm. Four years after his teacher, frightened by the tumult of the crowd, had run from his apartment (and, soon after, from Trieste and his pupil's life), he was eyewitness to a new historical twist. On a grey November afternoon, Italian troops disembarked in the port of Trieste. And not too long after this, a new set of spectres appeared on the streets. Young men from Italian suburbs and small towns marched about in black uniforms singing of youth and springtime; they beat their political opponents, and set fire to a large building in the centre of town – the Slovenian National Hall. When firefighters came to fight the blaze, they cut their hoses to the sounds of bellicose slogans. The young lawyer tried to settle down in the midst of the blind tumult of history. He opened a law practice, continued to read in philosophy and science, but he could not evade the angry times so characteristic of beaten Europe, the passionate crowds that gathered beneath the balconies or the pursuit of the secret police. He found himself among those educated Slovenians of Trieste who organised anti-fascist resistance. In 1930 he was warned that his arrest was imminent. He escaped over the border into Yugoslavia, and in a single day found himself in a new city among new people. In the thick fog that curled through the streets of Ljubljana that autumn, his inner vision searched for the far-off and now lost shining disk of Trieste's sun, and his inner ear listened to the howling of an Adriatic storm. With a beating heart, he read newspaper accounts of the convictions of his fellow Slovenes, whom the fascist courts sent to distant Sicilian prisons or to local villages under armed guard. There was something about this agitated time, this agitated atmosphere, that his analytic mind could not understand. He told his friends that when reading accounts of these political trials he sometimes felt a kind of emptiness in his head, something like what used to happen when he had to describe the details of a lamp for his teacher Joyce.

6.

It was to the light of a completely different lamp, a modern and electric one in the quiet reading room of the university library, that, in the middle of January 1941, he was leafing through the English newspapers which regularly carried accounts of the latest trials in Trieste. His glance was suddenly halted and numbed by a story from which he learned that James Joyce had died in Zurich. He was surprised to discover from this article that his former English teacher, the interesting and to his lawyerly mind somewhat eccentric professor Zois, had become a rather well-known writer in the intervening years. He resolved to read his books and wondered where he would get hold of them, since the author was practically unknown here. He did not know that he would soon find them where they were quite popular – in England.

But now was not a time for reading; events followed one after another, history thickened. There was great agitation among immigrants from Trieste, for all of them knew what awaited them if Slovenia was taken by Italian troops.

As in November 1918, in the spring of 1941 he again observed the arrival of their forces. This time the army did not disembark. Now they rolled in, and through the dusty streets of Ljubljana came motorised divisions, infantry and horses dragging artillery pieces, the barrels of which never fired a shot during the campaign of conquest. For the army of the country they rolled through had disintegrated all by itself.

By the time officers of the Italian secret police knocked at his apartment door, he was in Switzerland, taking a tram along the narrow and peaceful Zurich street up the hill to the cemetery. While his Ljubljana apartment was being turned upside down, he was standing at the grave of his former English teacher. Professor Zois, he said, and he could hear his laugh and see him as he stepped to the window and looked out at the sea.

There was no sea here, but far below was Lake Zurich, and it seemed to him that he could also hear that howling of the storm outside his window, winds that carried up to him the roar of the crowds in the harbour. But down below no troops were disembarking; tourists were getting off boats on to the wooden pier.

When, several days later, he got on to the train in Zurich that was to take him to Paris, an Italian court was convening in Ljubljana. In a session that took less time than did his trip to the French border, he was sentenced to death in absentia.

7.

In May of that same year, he was dropped off at his hotel by a Serb, a representative of the Yugoslav government in exile in London. Sirens were wailing on that warm and peaceful evening. His driver jumped into the car and drove off quickly, together with his suitcase. People were running on the street, and a man with a band on his sleeve pushed him into a bomb shelter. In the basement he heard the echoes of explosions, and through the basement window he saw a piece of glowing sky. Incendiary bombs were falling on the city beneath the vault of an evening May sky. Somewhere close by, the piece of glowing sky that he saw was marked by the bright lines of anti-aircraft fire. Then it turned out that the man who was standing next to him and calmly smoking a cigarette was the receptionist at the hotel he was supposed to stay in. The receptionist said that once again there would be no electricity, and that they would again be using kerosene or oil lamps. In that London basement, in the midst of an air raid, Joyce's pupil rocked with irrepressible laughter. He asked the receptionist to tell him how a lamp like that worked. The man was not surprised at the question, for his job was such that he had heard everything. So he lit another cigarette and began to explain. And thus he spent his first London evening, until the attack had ended, with that receptionist yielding to the descriptive passion, hearing about the workings of oil lamps, which turned out to be a bit different in London from Trieste.

He fell asleep in his small hotel room towards morning, fully clothed on his bed. While he slept, he dreamed that he was diving into the ocean near Trieste.

8.

His voice became famous in Slovenia. It was the voice of Radio London. His words were clear and determined, a call for resistance. He spoke of the German defeats in Africa and in Russia. He announced the landing in Sicily, narrated the battle for Monte Cassino and, with triumphant satisfaction, proclaimed the capitulation of Italy. His voice, emanating from radio speakers, was listened to after curfew behind shuttered windows in city apartments, while the muffled steps of German night-watchmen echoed through the streets. The partisans in liberated territories listened to him; their adversaries could hear him as well. His speech entitled "Plain Speaking from London" was printed as a pamphlet and dropped from Allied planes over Slovenia in 1944. Here he called on the Slovenian homeguards to join the partisan resistance. In the Slovenian press, which appeared with the approval of the occupation authorities, he was called the bawler from London.

By now he had been completely swallowed up by the whirlwind of history. One evening when, exhausted, he was shuffling papers in the London studio by the light of a desk lamp, he told a colleague that he would return. He would join the partisans. His colleague warned him that everything there had been taken over by the communists, but the bawler from London rebutted him sharply. On that very evening the colleague wrote in his wartime diary: *He is an honourable and sincere person I think, but hopelessly naive.*

By February 1945, he was on territory liberated by the partisans, and a few months later he was back in Ljubljana. When new people took power, he was named dean of the law school. Two years later he was arrested.

9.

"With a little bit of imagination," the interrogator said, "one could say that it was that James guy (or whatever you call him) who got you into this whole mess." Joyce's pupil was sitting at a table, a glowing shaft of pale light poured into his wide open eyes. A lamp was on the table, its powerful electric light illuminated his whole face. The red end of a lit cigarette circled behind him, and it moved in rhythm with the laughing lips from which emanated puffs of white smoke. "He taught you English," the investigator laughed, "and had you not known English, you would not have become a British spy."

"I am not a spy," said Joyce's pupil.

"You are a spy," said the voice out of a cloud of smoke. He told him this every evening and every night. And they spent many nights in that dark room, in the blinding circle of light through which the white traces of cigarette smoke could be seen. "You frequented the English consulate," he said. The light was white and sharp, and circles burned in his eyes. Joyce's pupil recalled the oil lamp, and its circle of warm, yellowish light. "We're finished," said the interrogator. "Now you can go back to your cell. Tomorrow you'll go to be shaved, and then to trial."

"I am not a spy," said Joyce's pupil.

"You are a spy," came the voice from behind the circle of light; "you are a traitor. And you will be sentenced to death."

Joyce's pupil went pale. It seemed to him that he could hear the roar of the sea whipped up by an Adriatic storm.

"I was sentenced to death once," he said quietly.

"That was in absentia," laughed the interrogator; "this time you will be present."

10.

That was on a hot July evening in 1947. They led him through a labyrinth of corridors and doors, each of which closed behind him. Back to his cell, as narrow as a closet – six paces long, two wide. All night long a light burned high on the ceiling; its red light danced in his eyes through his rough blanket, preventing him from sleeping. Behind that brightness, in his inner vision which was hidden from the light, deep in his head, in deep where time and space could be conquered, he saw a series of agitated images of Trieste piers, foggy Ljubljana streets and even foggier London streets.

Towards morning, towards the bright July morning that somehow managed to penetrate through his somnambulous state, he heard footsteps and loud voices from the street outside. The city streets were just beyond the walls of the Ljubljana prison, and people were heading to work. He got up just as he heard keys rattling. The barber was at the cell door. The boom of footsteps and voices multiplied outside, growing ever louder, a murmuring multitude of humanity. Around the court building, a crowd of righteous people was gathering to express their solidarity with the prosecutors who, in the name of the people, were about to begin the trial of the traitors, turncoats, spies and enemies.

From the waiting room he looked out on to a sea of heads which were being moved back and forth by an invisible force, some kind of invisible and inaudible wind. For an instant he saw himself and his teacher; that was the last image before they led him into the hall: they were standing by the window of his Trieste apartment, he was twenty years old and a crowd outside was yelling and hurling rocks at the Italian consulate. His teacher no longer had any kind of descriptive passion, and he was afraid – he wanted to run away, and he ran away. The pupil had laughed. Now it was July 1947 and he was not laughing. Now he was afraid – he too would have run away. But there was nowhere to go. There was only one way, and it led through a labyrinth of corridors and doors into the law court.

11.

All of the accused looked like shadows. They were worn out, they hadn't slept and they were worried. The hall was filled with people who greeted them with an ominous murmur. They were seated on the front bench, and arrayed behind them and along the walls were uniformed guards. The stenographers waited with their hands on their knees. Sharpened pencils lay on the desks, motionless as loaded guns.

The trial lasted for two weeks, from morning until night with a break for lunch. The sharp speeches of the prosecutors and the stammering of the accused were broadcast out on to the square in front of the courthouse and into other squares and streets throughout Ljubljana. All over the country, working people gathered around radio speakers and listened to the thunder of the prosecutor's speeches: "Some part of the Slovenian intelligentsia has always been in foreign service. They have always sold themselves and been hopelessly fascinated by things foreign, especially foreign money."

Full-page articles in the newspapers described the trial: *Nothing has brought so much unhappiness, blood, martyrdom and suffering to the people as has this small reactionary clique. Naked treason in the pay of foreigners is in the dock. They are being tried not merely by working people, but by all men, by all humanity*, wrote the *Slovenian Courier*.

On the sixth or seventh day, the prosecutor deposed

Joyce's pupil. He spoke of the book *Animal Farm* that the accused had received from England. According to the prosecutor, he had made vile use of his knowledge of English, acquired in Trieste, to translate excerpts from this loathsome pamphlet, and he had lent the book to his fellow conspirators. A hush fell when he asked the accused to describe the contents of this book. The hush radiated out through the microphones to the crowd in front of the law court. His silence gaped through the radio speakers, and the next day a newspaper described it as the poor and tortured silence of an impenitent man. At last the accused spoke. "Describe it...," he moaned, "I can't describe it. In my head..." he said.

"In your head?" shouted the prosecutor.

After a long pause the accused added, "In my head there is a kind of emptiness."

"As he himself asserts, there is an emptiness in his head," the prosecutor said calmly and triumphantly. And the people in the hall stirred, laughter coursed through the square in front of the court, the entire crowd began to applaud the prosecutor's words, as the daily news reported in big headlines the next day.

Beneath a lamppost to which a microphone was attached, an old man leaned over to his wife. "If he hadn't been moaning so, I'd say that his voice was familiar," he said. "Isn't that the bawler from London?"

12.

On August 12 the chief justice announced the verdict. The three accused were sentenced to death by firing squad, with confiscation of all their property and permanent loss of political and civil rights. The hall applauded. From the face of one of the judges, it could be seen that he was sickened by the applause. He lifted his hand to quiet the people, but when the hall calmed down, one could hear applause like an echo from the outside and then loud approval from the gigantic square which had been occupied from early morning by a crowd of people that had gathered to hear the announcement of the verdict.

13.

When they brought him to his cell, a piece of paper awaited him. They told him that he could write home or to whomever he wished. He lay down on his bed and looked up at the ceiling. That evening they turned out the light, for the first time in many months. Guards looked into his cell at intervals.

14.

He lived for the next two years in solitary confinement, although he was allowed to read there. Sometimes, late at night, his former interrogator came to sit by his bunk. One night he asked whether he thought that from a strictly juridical point of view his punishment had been just. He did not answer, just turned to the wall. Another time his nocturnal visitor wanted to know what had happened during the trial. Why had he not described the contents of the book, where had the sudden emptiness in his head come from?

"It is all because I do not possess the descriptive passion," said the former law school dean. The interrogator gave him a strange look, worriedly shaking his head.

Toward the end of the next year, he was told that he had been amnestied. Instead of the death penalty, he had been sentenced to twenty years in prison. Four years later he was paroled because of heart trouble. He settled down in a small upland city. All night a light burned in his window. In the mornings he looked up at the shining, white alpine peaks. He spoke rarely, and his movements were slow and unnatural.

15.

One evening in late autumn 1953 he heard footsteps and commotion in front of his house. He turned off the desk lamp, walked to the window, lifted up the curtain, and at that instant he felt an icy shudder course through his entire body. A dark clump of people was outside, and they were preparing to do something. Someone called out his name. Someone shouted: "He wants to sell Trieste to the Italians! He and his English friends." Blows rang out against the door, grumbling male voices were in the foyer, and a moment later they were in his room, which was immediately filled with bodies, with the smell of sweat and alcoholic fumes.

Powerful hands grabbed him and pulled him out of the house and on to the street. They loaded him on a wheelbarrow. The wheelbarrow bounced on the pavement on its way down to the river.

The procession was accompanied by bursts of laughter and shouts: "Speek Eengleesh, speek Eengleesh!"

The iron wheel of the wheelbarrow bounced on the pavement, the helpless body flew up like a sack, and the professor felt that his weak heart was going to stop. With shaking hands he tried to shield his eyes from the faces that leaned over him, from the mocking and the senseless hail of curses: "You old fool, old fool. Judas, traitor."

Whenever the wheelbarrow stopped to allow the man pushing it to spit into his palms before beginning again, lips spewing alcoholic vapours bent down to him: "Where are your English friends now?" And the question was answered by the yodelling laughter of women, and the grumbling guffaws of men: "Speek Eengleesh, speek Eengleesh."

16.
Before the iron wheel of the wheelbarrow set off down the street again, before the ecstatic procession could start up, the old man lifted his arms and fluttered his hands, trying to tell them something. As if he himself had finally understood

something. The shaking after this fluttering produced even more humourous smirks.

And even before they reached the river bank, their cheers, snarls and guffawing laughter had turned into a distant roar. That roar resounded in the same emptiness that took over his head like a black hole, like the impossibility of further description. Now it seemed to the professor that with his juridical brain and his analytic passion he had finally come to understand the meaning of the emptiness that appeared in the face of the impossibility of description. That is why his helpless body no longer felt the rain of mockery that was falling on him, did not take in the hail of curses which beat on him, did not react to the flood of laughter that broke over him and did not hear the stream of furious insults. That is to say, the monotonous and distant roar took place outside of his head and its emptiness, its hollow space. It was, in fact, no longer the meaningless roar of ever new crowds which wailed and howled like an Adriatic storm through the streets of Trieste to the sea. It was an approaching roar. And in the distance, in some endless space, it grew out of a single word, a word neither Slovenian nor English that had never been written down in any language, a word that had never been spoken or used to describe anything, a word that could say everything although neither teacher nor pupil could utter it, a word comprehensible in its incomprehensibility, but one that neither teacher nor pupil would ever be able to use. This was what he would have wanted to tell his former teacher, for he had come to understand that there is a word at the beginning and the end, and that that word has nothing to do with the language in which it is spoken or written.

That is why he fluttered his hands, and why the uplanders laughed even more joyfully and shouted even more loudly: "Speek Eengleesh, speek Eengleesh."

He no longer heard them, only the distant roar, and he didn't know by now whether it was the booming of the sea, or of the crowd, or whether it was the storm itself outside his windows amidst whose gusts could be heard Professor Zois's monotonous voice describing an oil lamp.

Translated by Andrew Wachtel

An Incident in a Meadow

The incident, which changed the life of the assistant professor Michail Shevchenko occurred in the middle of a bright sunny morning at the edge of a green meadow between the economics and the humanities departments.

The previous night the pain he knew so well had come back. It started in the evening with moderate pecking in his gums, with sensitive responses to the flow of his blood and beating of his heart. He knew it was coming, so he swallowed two pills, went to bed and tried to go to sleep between the flashes of the TV screen, in front of which his wife was sitting, like any other evening, senselessly switching channels. She also knew what was coming, so she considerately turned down the volume, but the picture kept jumping and crackling and stealing the sleep he so desperately wished for. However, he managed to fall asleep for a short time, and when the drilling pain woke him up, iridescent light was still sparkling from the screen. He knew the night was going to be long and sleepless. The desperately aching hollow incisor, third from the left at the top, started with its regular, and then more and more irregular painful rhythm to push, drill, painfully pierce under the cheek, through the tissues of the eye, towards the brain. His sleepless mate applied compresses to his face, which he pressed to his skin with nervous gestures, and then with angry thrusts pulled away and threw around the room. He awaited the first light of day feeling dizzy from the pills which did not work, with the brain shredded by pain, with delirious eyes. In this condition, at the moment when there was really no other way out, he decided he would go to the dentist.

Michail Shevchenko was convinced that the communists were to blame for his horrible and repeated toothaches, just as they were to blame for everything bad, unpleasant and unhappy in his life. Although his fate was his alone, and therefore totally unique, it was nevertheless one of the well-known and closely related stories, described in books, articles and essays in different ways. When he told American people the story of his trivial dispute with the authorities in his repressed and unredeemed country, about the dispute which had taken him to prison, about the escape and sanctuary he found in this free country, they politely nodded, and he knew he could no longer shock anybody: the story in itself and as such was common knowledge. He alone knew what all that meant: not only suffering – it was long past now – but life here, adopting a new civilisation, learning a new language, studies at university, where he, a grown up and accomplished man, had to sit shoulder to shoulder with bored and careless students. He endured it all, and he knew why. Having obtained a reasonable scholarship with the help of an emigrant organisation, he had gritted his teeth.

He managed to get a post as an assistant professor at an eminent university, and quickly proceeded from one exam to another. He gritted his teeth when they did not ache. And they ached more and more frequently. He managed to overcome all the fears and traumas implanted within his soul in his past life with inner discipline, but he found no strength, means or remedy to fight the piercing, repeated pain in his teeth. He had ruined his teeth a long time before in a prison at the other side of the ocean; that is, others had ruined them with bad food, shortage of vitamins, constant draughts, brushing with cold water. They had also implanted a deep and invincible fear of dentists. Whenever he thought of the prison butcher, his forceps and drills, darkness fell in front of his eyes. Actually not darkness, but red and black, because when the swollen prison quack was lacerating him, through the mist he looked alternately at his face and at a red poster with bold black letters on the opposite wall. He could never forget the poster, just as he could not forget the fat drills. He knew they had different equipment here. His wife and friends tried to persuade him. Day after day, they brought him brochures about turbo devices with drills turning at such high frequencies that the whole procedure was proven utterly painless; they told him of the gentle injections and tender hands of fair-haired women-dentists; but Michail Shevchenko, who dared oppose the terror of a huge communist empire, its army and secret police, one and the same Michail Shevchenko could not conquer his only fear, that of the squeaking of drills, the metal breaching of enamel.

And yet, that morning, with his brain shredded by pain, feeling dizzy from the painkillers, when he, with delirious eyes, looked at the red rising globe which reminded him of sunrises in his country, that morning it seemed he would finally make it.

Moaning, he carefully rinsed his aching mouth, slowly put on clean clothes, scrupulously tied his tie, and then, with a hammering heart, stood in front of a mirror. He heard his wife in the adjoining room making an appointment for him on the telephone. A thousand revolutions per second, he thought, a thousand turbo silent painless drills and more.

With peaceful and resolute steps, he walked along the faculty of economics. He knew a green meadow was awaiting him round the corner, stretching all the way to the building housing the humanities, and at the other side, round the next corner, to the bright windows of the consulting rooms, reflecting the strong morning sunlight. He liked the meadow at that hour; it reminded him of a region in his homeland which he had had to leave, of weeping willows by a stream flowing through a meadow. Despite the merciless pain, or probably because of it, he thought of his distant, forsaken country.

At the moment he stepped round the corner, two things happened. He perceived the expected large, green, sunlit stretch of grass. At the same time, by the edge dividing the grass and the pavement, between the open landscape and the wall of the faculty of economics, he noticed three or four stalls he usually avoided. Left-wing students displayed Marxist literature, counter-imperialistic pamphlets, sold T-shirts with pictures of Che Guevara, Marx and other bearded heroes. He probably would have ignored them, walked past them without looking at the group of young people who always hung around there. He probably would have, just as he always did, quickened his pace and become absorbed in the grass, greenery, chlorophyll, soft steps, memories, soil, which gave way under his feet like a cushion. He would most probably have done anything but what he actually did, his life would have unrolled in a completely different way, had he not on that unfortunate morning had a toothache, had he not spent a terrible night, had his brain not been shredded by pain, his body wobbly and his eyes sore with delirium.

A black-haired student with a scarf round his neck was

handing out leaflets; passers-by were taking them and shoving them into their pockets or reading them as they walked. Some simply skimmed through and dropped them in the nearby bin; others approached the stalls with leaflets in their hands. An ordinary scene which Michail Shevchenko knew well and which he gave a wide berth every morning. Maybe he stepped too close, maybe the leaflet dealer picked him out deliberately. Whichever, suddenly he was walking by his side, offering him a red, burning red sheet, imprinted with bold black letters. Michail Shevchenko simply waved his hand and speeded up his steps. But that morning, unlike any before, the young man walked after him, shoulder to shoulder with him, handing him that paper. He even waved it, so it seemed to Shevchenko: he quite violently brandished it right in front of his face. He stopped and looked the young man in the eye.

"I don't want this paper," he said.

"You don't have to take it," the young man said. "This is a free country."

"That's why I won't take it," said Shevchenko.

"You don't have to take it," said the boy with the scarf. He said it but did not move away. He kept standing in front of Shevchenko, pushing the leaflet ahead. Not ahead, into him, towards him, into his face.

The pain from the incisor, third from the left at the top, started pecking. He wanted to push the boy aside and continue his walk. But he did not push him aside. He moved away from him and let him stand there with a bunch of leaflets in his hand.

"Hey," shouted the black-haired Marxist from the depths of Latin America. "Hey, mister," he cried. Shevchenko did not look back. He was walking towards the orange light of the examination room windows. The pain was forcing its way through his cheek bone towards his eye. The young man came running after him.

"You might be interested in this one," he said and shoved a red piece of paper into his nose, so that Michail Shevchenko was not sure whether it was not the same one as before.

"I told you I was not interested," Shevchenko said and clenched his teeth, so that the pain rushed through the tissue of his eye.

"You said it about the other leaflet," the student said, "not this one."

The student later claimed that Michail Shevchenko had attacked him at that very moment. Shevchenko, however, in the discussions that followed, claimed he had done it later, that the student was the first to breach the rule of untouchability and academic and personal integrity.

As a matter of fact, Shevchenko was not absolutely positive as to who touched whom first, but he remembered distinctly that he wanted to move away once more. He moved to the left and touched the student with his shoulder, or else the student touched his hip. In any case, he took a few more steps towards the windows after the event. Their orange colour glittered in the sun so strongly that he put his sunglasses on. But, when he reached into his pocket for the glasses, he pulled out the red leaflet with them. Between fighting or ducking, the student had skilfully pushed it into his pocket. The orange windows shimmered. The pain was cutting through the tissue of his eye and towards the brain with a thousand revolutions. With turbo rotations it broached the membrane of the brain, it drilled and it revolved, just like the turbo drills revolved behind those windows, breaking the enamel, just like a fat drill a long time before had lacerated his jaws in a prison medical room, so that the inside of his skull roared and pieces were scattered around his mouth. He stopped. He turned. The student was still standing in the middle of the meadow with a bunch of red papers in his hands. He stepped towards him. The other simply stood there, smiling. He stepped towards him with clenched teeth, crumpling the piece of paper in his hand. The witnesses concealed this detail, this crucial detail. Only then did he step towards the student with the crumpled ball of paper in his hand. The smile on the student's face froze. He stepped aside.

"This is a fr..." he said. He probably wanted to say: "...ee country." But he only said: "...try." He could not say anything else because Shevchenko had shoved the ball right in between his teeth. Between his clenched teeth, but he grabbed him by the nape with the other hand and was pushing the ball through his lips, teeth, the healthy, pain-free, white Latin revolutionary teeth. Shevchenko saw people running across the grass towards them, but it was too late; he could not let go, he could not stop. He came to a few moment later, when they pulled him away from the young man, and when they both, shaking, looked at each other, uttered incomprehensible sentences, when they did not quite know what had happened. At all events, the assistant professor Michail Shevchenko had some blood on his knuckles, according to the witnesses. He thought the transparent red stain was not blood, but ink from the leaflet. Nobody carried out an analysis. Blood or not, the incident was inconceivable; the academic and civil freedom of speech was severely breached.

It was a scandal, by every standard. The following day a special issue of the student paper came out, with a huge title on the front page: "Who is Stopping Our Mouths?" Next to it was an awkwardly drawn caricature of a student with a paper ball between his teeth. At the humanities department, a meeting was called about academic freedom. Abusive posters appeared. The local TV station reported about the affair on the midday news. The professors of a famous university convened at a special conference. Assistant professor Shevchenko was not present because he had toothache. He sent in a written report about the incident, in which he tried to prove that the student started the violence by shoving the leaflet into his pocket after he had politely refused it. He did not speak about his attitude towards freedom. Or about his toothache. The dean telephoned and explained to him that everything had gone too far, that he knew about his past, but it could not justify the incident. That he should change universities, his job or himself, if he could.

Shevchenko changed everything. He handed in his resignation. He moved. He found a job as a reviewer with an insurance company. He worked exclusively at night. The job was badly paid and uninteresting, but it was solitary and quiet. That was all he wanted: solitude and peace. The following years he reviewed insurance materials at night, and during the day went to a park, where he spent long hours sitting by a stream where weeping willows grew. He pulled out the hollow incisor himself, third from the left at the top. His gums became inflamed, but his wife cured them with camomile tea her relatives had sent from the homeland.

On Saturdays and Sundays, when there were no reviews to be done, he tried to sleep, since the split afternoon sleeps were not worthy of the name. His wife, who every night senselessly switched channels on TV, often had to get up and with energetic jolts put a stop to his moaning, sometimes even screaming. Michail Shevchenko did not moan because of the pain in his tooth, cheek bone, eye or brain. His dreams were always the same. The prison quack from his distant homeland kept leaning over him. When he moved,

Shevchenko could see a red poster with bold black letters on the opposite wall. The features on the quack's face became more and more similar to those on the face of a black-haired boy with a scarf round his neck.

Translated by Lili Potpara

A Tale about Eyes

We have before us two stories about the overwhelming impression produced in a person when he looked into the eyes of a man he admired.

The first is the account of Kurt Erich Suckert, who is bathed in a clear and natural ray of light, reminiscent of the best Impressionist canvases, when he meets Ante Pavelić: "At first glance I saw only the bright gleam of his eyes, like the shimmer of a river's surface."

The second is that of Henry Abrams, whose ophthalmologist's subtle knowledge is overwhelmed by an inability to suppress a certain quavering, practically divine realisation as

---

Ante Pavelić (1889–1959) was the leader and founding member of the Croatian Ustasha fascist movement which was placed in charge of the Independent State of Croatia by the Axis powers in 1941. The Ustache were expelled by the communist Yugoslav partisans and the Red Army in 1945.

he recalls a glance into the blue eyes of Albert Einstein: "His eyes were angelic. You had the feeling that they knew everything in the world."

We have before us two scenes.

In the first, the object of interest is a bowl on a desk. The bowl is filled with some kind of small, spherical fruit. In the dim light they look like grapes or currants, but they aren't grapes or currants. The office is so small that the visitor has to sit with his back practically against the door. Behind the desk, which occupies almost half the room, sits a man in a uniform. The two sit eye to eye, as it were. Green light, the reflection of green trees on the hillside, filters through a window that looks out on to a square. The cramped room seems even smaller than it is because of the languid movements and warm serious voice of the man behind the desk, in whose eyes the visitor can see the shimmer of a green river. The man takes the bowl in his hands and pushes it across the polished surface of the desk. The visitor, who had initially thought that the bowl contained some kind of fruit, grapes or currants, now realises with a horror that threatens to overcome him that the spheres in the bowl are human eyes, gouged or cut out of their sockets. The year is 1942, and the visitor is Kurt Erich Suckert. Some two years later, even before the end of the war, his description of this scene (published under his pen name Curzio Malaparte) will become one of the blackest legends of our century. The story will find its way into other literary texts and, eventually, into histories. The office, the hands, the bowl filled with human eyes – all of these belong to the man in the uniform: Ante Pavelić. Everyone finds the scene convincing. No one doubts its truth, an illustration of Pavelić's horrifying proclivity to collect human eyes.

In the second scene we see hands that pick up a jam jar and bring it to eye level. The jar is filled with colourless liquid, probably formaldehyde, and on the bottom there are two small spheres. The hands shake the jar and the spheres move. They shake it again, and the spheres turn and slowly rotate in the embrace of the jelly-like substance, then come to rest again. The hands carefully place the jar back on the table, and the eyeballs sink to the bottom. Now they are facing up, and they gaze motionlessly at the man who had shaken them, right up close. The person stares dreamily at them. The scene takes place in complete silence broken only by the sound of cars on the road. He glances fixedly at the eyes that rest face up on the bottom of the jar, and they glance back at him. The jar contains a pair of human eyes. The room in which this silent confrontation takes place is neither a morgue nor the laboratory of some clinic. It is an apartment in a small vacation home in a godforsaken town somewhere on the eastern coast of New Jersey. The year is 1994, and the apartment, the hands, the jam jar and the eyes inside it are all the property of a man named Henry

Abrams. The eyes that stare up motionlessly at the owner of the jam jar are those of Albert Einstein. At the end of December of that year, pictures of the jar and the eyeballs will be beamed all over the world. But few will believe it; the scene will be considered an invention, an oculist's bizarre fantasy.

What is true in the first scene is the description of the Leader's office, the surroundings of Zagreb's Upper Town. True also is the description of the movements, voice and eyes of the man in the uniform if the shimmer of the green river in his eyes can be considered the truth. But Malaparte is a writer, and his truth is different. In an article he would write in the same year as his meeting with Pavelić (published in the Italian newspaper *Documento*), the sentences will radiate clever literary admiration. Ante Pavelić on the threshold of the office, tall, thin, with the grey reflection of the cold light of dawn on his face. "At first glance I saw only the clear reflection of his eyes," Malaparte writes, "the shimmer of a river's surface." Even the environment in which the Leader lived and ruled is described through the shining of human eyes. "The environs of Zagreb are full of music," he writes, "an architecture of green tones (green is the deepest colour). The presence of the Saya River gives nature an undertone of blue, a tender and firm glimmer. Something like the glint of human eyes." Curzio Malaparte admires the Leader's decisive manner, his unpretentious way of speaking, his modesty.

He writes about Pavelić's red cheeks, his muscular body, fleshy lips full of proud will and, again, about his deep eyes.

The writer accompanied the Leader on a trip to Monfalcone, and when they paused on the road between Ljubljana and Postojna, they saw a peasant couple working a patch of land amidst the rocks of the Karst. Pavelić speaks about the land, and Malaparte strives to remember every word. His love for the land is connected to "its tranquil, good, noble, and chaste dignity", he would write. "I began to understand," he writes, "that the mystery of Ante Pavelić is the mystery of extraordinary nobility, and that the land itself is mysterious, perhaps even more so than flesh and blood." Malaparte admires Pavelić.

At around the same time, at the other end of the world, the face of a great thinker was being observed by his private physician. During his eye exam, Einstein jokes, he gives his young friend life lessons. The young doctor, Henry Abrams, who is mentioned only in passing by Einstein's biographers as one among a number of intellectual friends, was the guardian of Einstein's health between 1939 and 1941. Guardian is a poor choice of words, however, for their relations really went in the opposite direction. Einstein was the guardian, and Abrams his ward. Relations between guardian and ward were marked by boundless admiration. Each time Einstein looked at him, the young Abrams got shivers down his spine. The eyes into which he glanced contained an entire universe of wisdom and knowledge. "His eyes," he would say years later, "were angelic. You had the impression that they knew everything in the world." It was, in fact, Einstein who pushed the young doctor to specialise exclusively in ophthalmology. After the war, Abrams did so, and several years later, now an eye specialist, he found himself at the same university, Princeton, in the same place as Einstein. Their friendship blossomed again in its original form. Abrams would visit the object of his admiration at home, where the two would talk for hours about everything except students. The guardian did his best to hook his ward up with a girl. And once a year Einstein would come to Dr Abrams' office for an eye exam. Here, too, there was no lack of admiration. "His eyes," Abrams would later say, "were as clear as crystal. They were endlessly deep."

In 1944, with a sudden and unexpected gesture of a type that was not uncommon in his life, Curzio Malaparte repudiated Ante Pavelić. The gesture in itself was not surprising, for the Leader's hour was passing and Suckert's political allegiances were shifting. What was surprising was its violence. He repudiated Pavelić with a violence more characteristic of a rejected lover, from a land that may be more mysterious than flesh and blood. In his book *Kaputt*, he describes Ante Pavelić as a cold-blooded criminal and sadist, a remarkable turnabout for this writer. And so he needed a huge, deep, fleshy, earthy, bloody metaphor with which to replace the shining eyes that glimmered like a river's surface. Where before there were shining eyes, now there are horribly gouged-out, horribly peaceful and silent gouged-out eyes of Serbs and Jews from concentration camps in the bowl on the desk, disembodied eyes that looked out into the dark silence of the office, eyes that would never again see green rivers and the architecture of dark green tones, green that is the deepest colour. And the notorious horrifying bowl on Pavelić's desk would feed the imagination of historians, writers and biographers. Whole generations would understand it as a metaphor for Ustashe crimes, and it would captivate their imagination as an example of the incomprehensible mystery of evil, which contains more mystery than flesh and blood, perhaps more mystery than the earth itself. Men of the pen and the mind would appear, and they would claim that they, too, with their own eyes as it were, had seen the bowl filled with gouged-out eyeballs that from a distance looked a bit like some kind of fruit although they were really human eyes that had been torn out by bayonets. Malaparte's bowl of eyes on Pavelić's desk would leave an immutable stamp on this century of evils, a judgement against that world and a judgement against the time of the *quattour hominum novissima*: death, judgement, hell and heaven. It would make no difference that Raffaele Casertano, an Italian diplomat who was present during the conversation between the writer and the Leader, denied the existence of the bowl. Equally useless would be the commentary of some sober individuals who would say that given the quantity of proof of the Ustashe's actual crimes, there is no need to invent anything. Malaparte is deep and mysterious. He sees the bowl filled with gouged-out eyes, and everyone else sees it clearly through his eyes.

When Dr Abrams heard that Albert Einstein had died, his life was transformed in an instant. The world in which he lived in close proximity to a person he worshipped had been destroyed. In fact, in his own words, it seemed that the world had ceased rotating: "I felt that the world had stopped." Later he would say that it was a stroke of luck that brought him to Princeton Hospital at that exact moment. Without having thought it through, he knew what he had to do: to save those eyes, the clearest crystal, the deepest and wisest. The whole thing took little more than twenty minutes. "I needed only scissors and tweezers," he would say forty years later. That very night in the morgue, Einstein's young friend first cut the optic nerve and sliced through the six connecting muscles. Very far back, he would say, so as not to damage the eyeball. Then he removed Einstein's eyes from their sockets with the tweezers and put them in a glass bottle. He poured liquid over them to prevent these treasures that would now belong to him from drying out. Later he would transfer the eyes to a different jar, and eyewitnesses would say that it was indeed a jam jar. And he would hide it in his home for the next forty years. When in December 1994, fearing in his old age that his secret might go with him to the grave, he made the true story public, no one wanted to believe him.

Abrams was a man of reason, and it was his devotion to reason that led him to the same type of action that motivated people in the Middle Ages when they cut the limbs off saints because they believed in their eternal divine power. Thus, he thought it reasonable to save the eyes which contained all the wisdom of the world.

Some years after the war, a Croatian writer recalled how during the war he happened to be invited to visit the headquarters of the Croatian government. He remembered, as if it was happening today before his very eyes, what occurred when by mistake he walked through an unlocked door in the Leader's quarters. There he saw something that made his blood freeze: on the desk was a bowl filled with eyeballs. When people who worked there at the time told him that he could not have seen anything of the sort, he angrily rebuked them. He hadn't just read about this but had seen it with his completely healthy eyes, and he was, at that time just as today, in full possession of his faculties. The Slovenian writer Vitomil Zupan, or at least his first person partisan hero, saw those eyes even earlier, immediately after the Ustasha had cut them out of their sockets. He sees them near a tiny village named Ogulin, from which they are to be sent to Zagreb, and writes about them in a short story entitled "Blue Eyes for Pavelić" that was published shortly after the war. An icy cold wind is blowing through the hills around Ogulin where a partisan patrol lies in ambush. The young hero thinks about the cigarettes that he will find in the pockets of the dead enemies, hoping for, as Zupan writes, "a comb made of bone, thin and long, with which he would comb his wet mane into a beautiful coif, as if in the city". After a tense wait, two passers-by appear with the letter U on their caps. The partisans kill the first one on the spot, but the other, "a real ox", is only wounded. A wild chase after the escaping beast ensues. Grenades litter the snow, the man is wounded, and he leaves a pool of blood with each step. Eventually he drops, riddled with bullets. In disgust the partisan looks at the flat, pocked face with its pancake nose and its open, round eye. He rifles through the pockets and finds a photograph showing the Ustasha holding a knife between his teeth; the knife is painted blood red. Then he opens the man's knapsack. "Inside were some three hundred and forty pairs of human eyes. The blue eyes were in a separate little bag." On the bag the Ustasha, "that ox", had written "in coloured pencil: blue eyes for Pavelić (girls')".

The Croatian writer's story and that of Vitomil Zupan serve as confirmation of Malaparte's description. And, more recently, chronicles and historical works have included it.

At the beginning of 1955, Albert Einstein began to suffer

ever more severely from what is called an abdominal aneurysm. On Saturday 16 April 1955, he began to complain of sharp pain all over his body. The pain was so strong that he passed out in his bathroom. He was taken to Princeton Hospital. His young friend Henry Abrams happened to be right by him at that time. There was no longer any possibility of looking into those crystal eyes and their vivid depths. The eyes were fading. Einstein's son was the last person to speak with him. They talked about politics and made some corrections to his last project, the unified field theory. On Monday, at 1:15 a.m., Einstein mumbled his last words. No one knows what he said. He spoke them to the nurse in German, and although she was, of course, listening carefully, she did not know a word of that language. When the ophthalmologist Abrams heard that his terrestrial god had died, it only took him an instant to decide to save those beloved eyes for humanity. At around four in the morning, he went to the morgue and there, with the specialised knowledge of an eye doctor, he was able to complete the job in some twenty minutes. In a sense, the New Jersey oculist felt that his twenty-minute act was a major feat. He gave Albert Einstein eternal life. "I felt," he said later, "that he could not die, that his eyes stood for all of his influence." Because they had been preserved, Abrams thought that the great man would now live for ever. From time to time, he thought of dissecting them, but the divine shiver that passed through him whenever he glanced at them caused him to change his mind. When he would finally show them to amazed reporters in 1994, he would say ecstatically, "You see, they look like new". A friend of Einstein asserts that the father of relativity frequently said that he wanted to be cremated so that after his death people would not be able to come and rummage among his bones. And that is what was done. After a modest eulogy attended by only a dozen or so mourners, the old man's ashes were scattered, just as he had wished, no one knows exactly where but probably over the Delaware River. The mourners who were followed by his glance (which slid over the surface of the river) would probably have been robbed of the tranquilising vision of ephemerality had they known that his eyes, the instrument and vessel of his glance, were hidden in jam jar.

After the war, during a talk in Athens, Malaparte admitted that the story about the bowl filled with gouged-out human eyes on Pavelić's desk was an invention. When he was asked why he had made it up, he laughed quickly and added: "It's all the same whether they were human eyes or grapes or currants. I wanted to achieve an effect, and you can't feed the imagination on currants." The astonished silence that ensued proves only that the imagination had indeed fed on those currants, and that the imagination had already turned them into the actual dead eyes of our century. Eyes which, with their silent glance, also speak about the living eyes of

Ante Pavelić with the shimmer of a green river, about those eyes which contained an unusual and sensitive power, as the very same author wrote. Such was this power that the writer subordinated his voice to it. As it is said in the Bible: *I try to make you love me, for your eyes are over me, your servant.* And such was this power that Kurt Erich Suckert, with the same mysterious earthly passion that had once possessed him, gouged out those eyes, multiplied them and put them in a bowl in his famous account.

And in a similar way somebody else, Henry Abrams (now an old timer, but a young man when he cut them out) possesses eyes that send divine shivers down his spine. In an apartment on the east coast of New Jersey, the wrinkled but once upon a time smooth and dexterous hands of Henry Abrams clumsily pick up and shake the jam jar. In his opinion, it contains a relic more precious than those in the Cathedral of Cologne. His hands touch the glass top of the jar that contains the spheres covered with liquid and moves it toward his own once flexible but now somewhat weak eyes. The spheres slowly sink to the bottom where they come to rest side by side, and they look quietly and motionlessly at the person who finds love and knowledge in them and a great deal more besides. For, as he said, when you look into those eyes, you see all the beauty and mystery of the world.

It is said that after he looks at them for a long time he puts the eyes into a bag and takes them by car to a storage facility an hour away. He wouldn't want anything unexpected to happen to them.

That could easily be the end of the tale. And what do we really have in our hands that made it worth the telling? An old oculist who drives some eyes, carefully preserved in formaldehyde, down some empty road in New Jersey. A bowl filled with currants and Suckert's short laugh from which a fantasy grows. We have two stories and two scenes. We can only sense the link between them, but we can't fully grasp it. We suspect also that the eyes stored in the secure vault know what is happening to them. And so did the real or invented eyes in the bowl on the desk in the darkened room of that war year. That suspicion is exasperating, but a horrible allure that gives birth to further stories grows from it, although nothing is certain here. The only sure thing is that somewhere there are eyes even more angelic, eyes that know even more, whose gleam is even stronger than the green shimmer of a river's surface. And the vision of those eyes accompanies us. They alone know where the end of a tale is and what will happen even before a reliable end is reached.

Translated by Andrew Wachtel

Aethiopica, Repetition

In May 1945, in the hills of Slovenia, a military unit missed the destination the commander had marked on the map the night before in the light of a torch, and after a night's march found themselves above an unknown village. The glimmer of early morning light penetrated through the branches and trunks of trees, blinding the men of the night. They stopped without being ordered to and with an instinctive feeling, stemming from years of fighting, hid behind trees and bushes. Spring sunlight poured over the warm landscape beneath them, and their eyes wandered upwards, hungrily swallowing the glittering of the distant snow-covered mountains over which they were bound. Their tired eyes moved away from the painful glare, drifted into the valley and stopped on the gentle slope above the forest. There, a white church tower was sticking from a rounded grass belly.

As they moved closer, they suddenly perceived a village below, with houses pressed to the hill, shyly gathered around the church. And they discerned an unusual, mysterious sight.

On the shingled roof of one of the houses, a flame was blazing. There was hardly any smoke, as if the light wood of the house had caught fire only a moment before. They could hear dry crackling, and the warm air above the fire shimmered in the clear morning light. It seemed that the fire would jump on to the neighbouring house any minute, and yet, apart from the dry crackle of the fire, no sound drifted from the village, no cry, scream, mooing of cattle, howling of dogs, no human or animal sound at all. Next to a house at the end of the village, on the road leading to the valley, stood a loaded cart. The two horses which were supposed to pull it lay motionless on the ground. As if somebody had wanted to harness them to take the load to the valley, but changed his mind at the last moment and killed them right in front of the cart. Some slaughtered pigs had been thrown on the cart, white sucklings lying like swans among the big ones whose dead meat hung over the edges, and above them trembled the black-brown feathers of slaughtered poultry. The cow must have been killed last. By the cart, on its own, somehow separated from it, lay its huge belly; the head was hidden below, as if it had climbed between the wheels in agony. The belly looked like an inflated yellowish balloon, and its legs were tiredly kicking into the air. The men stood up, forgetting their usual prudence, and stared in surprise at the silent scene below, the scene in which no living soul, or at least not fully alive, had appeared so far. One by one they looked down questioningly and at the bearded face of their commander, who still could not decide whether to retreat into the forest or descend into the village. He took a few steps forward down the slope, and then suddenly threw himself on the ground, pressed his face to the wet grass, and a split second later his men quickly lay down behind him, although they did not see what he had seen. The arms rattled with a metal sound for a moment, and then everything went silent again.

The commander thought he could discern human bodies lying around the houses.

For a long time they stayed like that, glued to the damp spring soil, listening intently to the crackle of the fire taking hold of the lower storey of the house; smoke started slowly coming from the inside. Then the commander crawled back. Together with his men, he moved back to the forest and stationed them along its edge, ready to fight or withdraw; he sent two men to look around. Like worms they squirmed down the slope without pausing for a single moment. The others held their breaths when they saw them rise and, in a crouching run, disappear behind a barn. A few more tense moments passed. Then they saw one waving his machine-gun, and they heard his incoherent screaming. All stirred at once and, weapons in hands, started moving towards the silent village, which in the morning sunlight appeared even quieter because of the crackling of the fire. The scene waiting for them there was even more mysterious. Incomprehensible and horrible, a dreadful sight even for soldiers used to all kinds of terror.

The bodies lying around the houses were corpses.

It could not have been long since these people had been killed, since some were dead, others were dying, and their limbs in their final convulsions testified that not much time had passed since the fight had ended. And clues on the battlefield suggested it could not have been a fair fight.

It was not a battlefield; no fight had taken place there. All the indications the unknown killers had left behind pointed to the fact that these people had been surprised, and that the horrible slaughter had happened very early in the morning, quite possibly at dawn, when some were still asleep or lying in their beds, while others had started doing their morning chores in kitchens or stables. The corpses were half dressed, as if they had been dragged out of bed a moment before. A half-naked woman was wrapped in a crumpled, blood-soaked sheet. The others looked as if they had been surprised during their morning work. An old man lay in the door of the stable, clutching in his dead bony fingers the handle of a fork he had obviously used to protect himself. The attacker was better skilled: he had cut his throat. By another corpse lay a dish full of polenta, still steaming. Somebody had tried to climb a barn; he was left hanging between the bars with a smashed skull. This was not an armed confrontation: not a single shot was fired; everything was done with blades and blunt objects; most of the bloody work was carried out with the knife. It seemed that the silent slaughter had taken place a very short time before. The army, which instead of reaching a previously defined destination had happened on this scene of human death by mistake, had not heard any shooting, although they had been very near; the most terrible things probably happened just as they were crawling through the forest towards the light, probably an hour before, when they had been resting in a basin behind the village for a while.

In a small square in front of the church which thus far had been hidden from their eyes, they saw ten corpses of young men, obviously selected for systematic execution, a bloody ritual sacrifice. The boys lay next to each other; probably all the boys in the village. Throats had been slit and blood was pouring from the wounds into vessels of different size and shape, overflowing with coagulating blood, which must have been collected from the houses by the bloody visitors, or else the boys had had to bring them along. It seemed designed by farmers with their peasant imagination. In this part of the world, this is how they slaughter pigs: they place a vessel under their throats so that the blood is not wasted.

The act pointed to the anger or even revenge of the slaugh-
terers, who had wanted to humiliate their victims even in
death, and probably leave a message of slaughter; the air was
heavy with the smell of blood and intoxicated lust. And yet,
despite the dreadful sight, nothing was clear. Nothing implied
what had caused the recent homicide; there was no one left
alive to tell the story. And it was not clear which of the
armies that had traversed these Slovene hills in this month
of May could have done it; there were no military signs, not
a cap, not even a button torn from the sleeve of the execu-
tioners by a victim in agony, nothing at all. There was a broken bottle next to the corpses, reeking of spirit. Not a very
enlightening clue. The cartload alone testified that they had
wanted to take away food: the slaughtered pigs and poultry,
the cow lying with a swollen belly by the cart, its head
beneath it, the cow they could not or did not have time to
load. All this led to the assumption that they had planned
to cook it in a huge military cauldron, and that the slaugh-
terers were a larger unit of an unknown army. They had left
in a hurry; even the horses intended for pulling the cart they
had killed at the last moment, slit their throats wide.

The reason for such a hasty departure was probably the
arrival of the unit confronted with the deadly scene; outly-
ing sentries had probably spotted them. Then there had come
a sudden command. The commander of the slaughtering
army possibly simply changed his mind after the work had

been done and left the dead animals behind in order not to slow down their immediate departure. War abounds in coincidences, motives triggering killing are always unpredictable, commands brisk and paradoxical. The chaos reigning in the hills of Slovenia in those days, in the hills where some armies advanced and others retreated, was unpredictable, full of sudden incentives followed by brisk decisions. And actions leaving questions, some remaining unanswered for ever. Therefore there was no reliable answer to any of the questions the soldiers asked themselves. In any case, they soon stopped asking questions altogether. *Although they did not know what had happened, they were tempted by the spoils: they simply granted themselves the right of victors and set to work.* Even before the commander gave permission, they searched the houses for things they could take. These things were of no use to the villagers; watches, which the troops liked most, do not tick for the dead, do not show the departing time.

And yet, not everybody was dead. A soldier taking a clock off the wall in a dark room of a village house suddenly heard a hiss. When he raised his eyes, he beheld a pair of glittering eyes in semi-darkness, and a moment later a cat, ravaged by fear, jumped into his face. The screaming mad beast then ran into the wall, into the doorpost, jumped over a couple of corpses in the street and disappeared behind the houses. And where the cat had disappeared, another living being emerged. An old, heavy horse in the meadow behind the church. He had a harness on, as if they had wanted to use it but it had fled, or else they had forgotten it, doing more important things. When the bearded soldiers tried to approach it, the clumsy old horse with big sad eyes suddenly became very agile. It reared so that the men stepped back, and then it turned and cantered towards the edge of the forest. There it stopped, turned its head and looked at the village, at the house by then almost completely eaten by flames.

In the vicinity of the burning house, which they dared not approach, two soldiers finally came across a living Christian soul. Two, in fact, but one was by all appearances already passing to the world beyond. A bloody trail led from the street into the house, as if somebody had dragged a heavy bloody load. When they entered the house, they momentarily forgot all about the trail. With skilled hands they threw things around to find anything useful before the fire destroyed it. But a second later they stopped dead. They heard movements on the upper storey and, when they listened more closely, human moans. The dark red trace they had noticed outside led up the wooden staircase. The stairs squeaked under their boots, and they heard another moan, of pain or fear of the coming steps. One of the soldiers carefully pinned a hand grenade with his teeth. At that moment, a young woman emerged at the top of the stairs, dressed in a white cotton gown in which she had gone to bed the night before, just when the commander was marking the destination on the map in the light of a torch. She stopped for a moment, looked at them with terrified eyes, and then disappeared inside. They rushed after her.

By her bed, slightly leaning on it, lay a young man covered in blood. He had a white cloth at his throat, which had turned red. He was still alive, just, since his eyelids opened and closed with difficulty; and he was dead, but not quite, since only the white eyeballs showed under his eyelids, the pupils disappearing into the eye sockets. And the young woman, who must have been beautiful when her hair was not disordered, her teeth clenched and her eyes delirious, the young woman stepped in front of him to defend him. From the row of the young men's corpses with slit throats, she had dragged him up here to protect him, to give him back his departing life. She was muttering fierce incomprehensible words, blurred groaning sounds. The two soldiers stepped back; they did not want to harm her. They listened to her groaning with surprise, for the sound was like the crying of the mad cat. They stood facing each other for a few moments. Two armed, bearded, dead-tired soldiers from the forest and a young woman, with everything she had seen that morning in her eyes, in hopeless defence of the dying young man, who was perhaps her lover.

The scene, which stayed alive in the memory of one of the two soldiers, the scene he described many years later, irresistibly brings to mind the beginning of Heliodorus'

Aethiopica. Furthermore, from the very beginning the scene looked as if it was meant to be repeated. The repetition of a human situation, which Heliodorus described in refined Greek in the third century AD: from the hills above the mouth of the Nile, men dressed like brigands descended. They watched the shore carefully, and their eyes rested on the glittering surface of the sea. Then they beheld an unusual sight. A loaded ship was tied to the shore, sinking deep with her burden, not a living soul to be seen on her deck or the shore. And the shore was covered in corpses. *It could not have been long since these people had been killed, since some were dead, others were dying, and their limbs in their final convulsions testified that not much time had passed since the fight had ended. And clues on the battlefield suggested it could not have been a fair fight.* The Egyptian brigands stared at the scene, which looked as though it had been left behind by an evil spirit: wine and blood, feast and slaughter, drinking and killing, offerings of wine and human sacrifice. All they could see were the defeated; the victors had disappeared. *Although they did not know what had happened, they were tempted by the spoils: they simply granted themselves the right of victors and set to work.* When they approached the ship and the corpses, they saw a new, even more mysterious sight. An incredibly beautiful young woman was sitting on a rock. "Deep sorrow poured over her face," says Heliodorus, "but pride and nobility radiated from her body." Before her lay a handsome young man covered in wounds. The girl, a laurel wreath on her head, placed her right elbow on her left leg and put her face in her hands. Her head held high she looked at the wounded boy. The image which was later called "classical pietà". At first the brigands were scared by the almost godly scene, and then they decided to take the girl with them and let the young man die. At that moment, the girl pointed a sword at herself and threatened she would kill herself if they did not take them both. The commander decided to save them both. And so in *Aethiopica* a new life started for the wounded Teagenes and beautiful Hariklea, and in the long story we read about everything their exciting life and the gods brought them. The author considered the act of the brigands' commander "worthy of praise". "A noble sight and a glimpse at beauty", he says, "must soften even the hard heart of a brigand and defeat brute force." And the reader gradually discovers God's economy in their story, as it is said word for word in the original.

God's economy in our story, which in many elements restates the opening scene in *Aethiopica* and happened in May 1945 in the hills of Slovenia, unfolds in a different way. From the scene which stayed alive in the memory of one of the two soldiers and which he described many years later, it quickly proceeds towards its denouement. No laurel wreath, no face in the palms, nobody noticed the nobility which would soften the hard heart of an armed man. A godly scene was not possible so many years later. Where in *Aethiopica* the story begins and takes its heroes into a new life, our story ends. The month is May, the year of our Lord is the merciless 1945.

So they stood facing each other for a few moments. Then the soldiers grabbed the girl, who muttered incomprehensible groans, kicked, bit, wet with tears and the boy's blood, they grabbed her, tore her away from him and pulled her to the square in front of the church. When they told the commander that somebody was still alive up there, he ordered them to bring him too. He could not be carried, so they dragged him by the legs and arms, his head with slit throat dangling on the ground. They dragged him along the same trail, exactly to the place where he had lain among the corpses of his fellow villagers. His pupils rolled in his eyes, he groaned through his cut throat, so that the cloth reddened with new blood; he whimpered hoarsely and gargled, as if he had realised where he was, saved a moment before, and now again among the lost. The girl, who a moment before was rigid with sadness, pulled away from the two soldiers with incredible force and threw herself towards him, on to the dead. Suddenly, nobody knew how, there was a knife in her hand. She hugged the dangling head of the young man with her left hand, pressed it to her bosom and brandished the knife at the two soldiers trying to step closer and in front of the commander's eyes undo what they had done in a moment of thoughtlessness. The commander waved his hand, gesturing to leave her alone. Then he stepped forward. He leaned over her and quietly whispered, "We won't hurt you; we don't want to do you any harm." When she had calmed down a little, it became clear in her delirious eyes that she had understood the words, but not their meaning. The commander moved even closer. Who was here, who had done this, he wanted to know. She shook her head and groaned. She pointed to the soldiers standing around. She pointed at him. She's mute, one of the men gathered around her said; in war, a new scene emerges every moment. And if there was an art historian among the soldiers, the narrator did not know it, he could not but think of the strange, distorted version of a modern pietà from May 1945.

"She's not mute," said the commander; "she's gone mad."

The man whose face the cat had scratched quickly added: "They are all mad here, even the cats." And the soldiers laughed loudly, to chase away the eeriness of her eyes and her finger pointed at them.

"Where did they go?" the commander shaped the question with his lips. "Just tell us where they went. There?" he pointed to the valley. "Or up?" he pointed to the hill.

She never uttered another sound. She dropped the hand with the knife and leaned over the boy's face so that she covered it with her long fair hair. A silent picture of deepest sorrow, no irresistible beauty, just sorrow. One of the soldiers, the one who told the story, turned away feeling something gathering in his throat – apparently it happens even to soldiers. They were all silent.

Somebody said: "We're not getting anywhere."

The commander said, "It's true. We're not getting anywhere."

He stood up. He stepped towards the stairs of the church where his bag and machine-gun lay. He sat down and spread the map on his lap. While looking for their missed destination, he was outlining a new itinerary and briskly giving orders. The soldiers scattered around the village and started loading the cart with provisions for the long journey across the mountains glittering in the snow and strong morning sun. They harnessed the horse – they had finally managed to catch it. The cart was too heavy and the horse too old, so they had to push with their strong shoulders before it moved. The cart ran over the throat of the cow with its rear wheel, so that it rocked dangerously. Then it moved quickly, since the road led downhill, towards the valley. The commander stepped after the cart, but, when they had left the village behind, suddenly stopped. He turned back towards the houses gathered around the church, towards the spiralling smoke coming from the ruin. He scratched his stubbled face and stared ahead for a moment. Then he waved his hand and one of the soldiers came running to him. The commander nodded towards the square. They could clearly see it from there, with its silent, mad witness. The girl in the white gown still held the boy's head in her lap. The commander's gesture implied that something had happened in God's economy of this story which did not lead to a repetition, but to the final end of something which had started there at an early hour, nobody knew how or why.

The horse with sad eyes slowly pulled the load along the road, easily now, because the slope gently descended. A soldier was running back and up. The knife he pulled from his belt glittered in the sun. Its reflection drifted towards the snowy mountains over which they were bound, and silently disappeared. The commander looked at the map. He did not want them to be lost again.

A Castilian Image

Something happened during Ulric's pilgrimage to Compostela, which the people from his entourage were unable to explain, and which changed the young count completely for a while. It was near Valencia, perhaps near a place called Sergoba, as some later claimed; in any case, it was in the middle of a hot day, in the middle of an undulating, baking-hot Spanish plain, when Ulric suddenly ran his horse towards a lonely chapel. A short while before, they had stopped in a grove on a gentle slope, from where one could, with a single glance, embrace the patches of red soil with white stones and sparse bushes scattered around. Between the trees on the slope casting shallow, weak shadows, they rested and quenched their thirst; they were tired, and only now and then exchanged a few words. They lay and sat, and in the silence which settled upon them, the only sound was the buzz of insects gathering from God knows where around the horses' flanks and muzzles. A horse loudly pissed into the softened soil; from somewhere came the metallic sound of a sword striking a shield. Far and around, no village could be seen; what was visible from the grove on the slope was only a torrid landscape, so that the tired eyes blinked into the glow. A single building stood not far from where they had stopped, at a winding pass on a hill that looked almost like the earth's back. It was a white chapel with an elongated nave and a belfry rising slightly above it, a belfry which resembled the head of a crouching white dove, which had flown from God knows where and, tired, sat perched on the back of the hot land. It was not clear why there was a belfry and a bell in that chapel, for whom it was supposed to toll and whom to summon to prayer, since there was no trace of human life to be seen far around. The men from the entourage knew that it was they who would pray if nobody else, for their master passed no temple without stopping; they rested there before prayer so that men and horses would not lie down, eat, drink, fart and piss around the holy place.

Ulric stood silent for a while at the edge, between shadow and light. Then he suddenly ordered his horse to be brought; he mounted it and slowly rode into the radiant landscape. It was in the middle of the undulating plain, in the Kingdom of Castile, perhaps near Valencia, not far from the place called Sergoba, as some later claimed.

In 1430, a mighty feudal lord, Hermann of Cilli, sent off two pilgrim expeditions with a military entourage consisting of knights, shield-bearers and pages. The one went on a pilgrimage to Rome, led by Hermann's sinful son, Friedrich, who had on his conscience the murder of his wife, debauchery and adultery, nauseating drinking and impertinent violence. The other was headed by Ulric, Friedrich's son and Hermann's grandson, a young count of a much more virtuous character than was granted to either his father or his grandfather, a man with a ruler's determination and audacity, on whom the old lord rested all his hopes. Ulric, chosen to be the bearer of a promise and blessing, to open up a firm future with his vow, undertook a much longer journey, to St James's in Compostela, in order to be purged. Chroniclers reported that the sudden piousness of old Hermann and his offspring attracted a great deal of attention. He had obviously realised that, for the future of the mighty dynasty, it would be useful to gain some help from God, in addition to money and soldiers, cunning and cruelty. The chroniclers also wrote that, over the last few years, Hermann had been getting up at night and wandering around with eyes filled with confused fear and terror. Of all the crimes he had committed, he was most haunted by the death of the young and sadly beautiful Veronica, his son's unhappy mistress, who was not destined to become a countess of Cilli; young Veronica, whom he had ordered to be killed, her own blood extinguishing the fire of those seductive eyes which had so alluringly ignited his son, as was also written. Thus many believed that the sudden devotion of the cruel old man, who could no longer undertake a pilgrimage – and had therefore sent off his son and his grandson – was a consequence of his unexpected remorse, which inevitably comes before death. Remorse for the night of the ruthless murder, for the sadly pretty face of Veronica, which rose before his eyes every night.

Friedrich's journey, as the chroniclers reported, proceeded in accordance with his turbulent nature, accompanied by constant difficulties on the way, conflicts with the nobility, townsmen and peasants, drinking and armed confrontations. Even before he reached his destination, Friedrich was captured at the border by the Count of Ferrara and kept prisoner, together with his debauched entourage, until bailed out and sent home before he completed his pilgrimage.

Ulric's pilgrimage was completely different. His expedition, which set off in the middle of winter, did not stop only in castles and towns, where it was warmly received, but also in villages with churches, settlements and solitary chapels in the hills. Even in front of the shrines at crossroads, Ulric often not only crossed himself but dismounted and knelt, or at least bowed his head and quietly said a prayer. Through Gorizia, northern Italy and southern France, the road of repentance led them to distant Compostela. The entourage admired their young master, who not once forgot himself either through debauchery, excessive eating and drinking, haughty behaviour or greedy acceptance of gifts. The count was always serene, he encouraged them in windy and rainy weather, he refused to be carried over dangerous mountain passes and walked with bleeding feet, like the others, next to the horses with foaming muzzles. While they were on the long journey, winter passed and spring came with the greenery of Italian and south French fields and meadows. They left behind the dead horses and sick pilgrims; they gazed at the blue sky near the Mediterranean, travelled through the warm rains of the Pyrenean mountain passes, and finally reached the glimmering brightness of the Spanish fields and rocky plains, and one day a grove on a slope where the silence was interrupted by the thin, hissing buzz of insects and the humming of field beetles, before a solitary chapel which all of a sudden changed Ulric completely.

Ulric stood silent for a while at the edge, between shadow and light. Then he suddenly ordered his horse to be brought; he mounted it and slowly rode into the radiant landscape. It was in the middle of the undulating plain, in the Kingdom of Castile, perhaps near Valencia, not far from the place called Sergoba, as some later claimed.

For an instant he vanished from sight, and then his figure, which had become one with the horse, reappeared in the valley, in the centre of the shimmering sunlight. And before he started ascending towards the white chapel, a few knights and pages rode after him; the others stayed in the grove. Ulric dismounted on top and, impatient, pushed the door, which would not open, looked around for help, and then charged at the wood with his shoulder; the door gave in and the dark interior gaped open. Ulric stopped for a moment, bowed his head, placed his hands together before him and entered. His eyes, aching with the light, at first saw nothing; he crossed himself and, instinctively, stepped towards the altar. Cold rushed through his body; his eyes gradually began to make out the contours of the wooden silhouettes and paintings on the wall. It was a modest chapel: the murals were faded, the paint had peeled off the wooden statues, and a weak light penetrated in a narrow beam through the windows high beneath the ceiling. Ulric knelt, lowered his eyes to the cold stone and started to pray.

When he looked up at the altar again, he heard at the same time the neighing of the horses outside the church and the thick droning of the insects coming from somewhere, from the foreign sea of the baking undulating plain which surrounded the nave. As he rose and slowly stepped towards the door, his eyes for an instant followed the ray of light falling vertically inside towards the baptismal font. And there, at the very same moment, he perceived a painting quite different from the others – alive, in bright colours, not the least faded like the rest, as if the painter had just finished his work. It

was the head of John the Baptist, a dead head in a living picture, an image which nailed Ulric to the ground, leaving
him immobile for a few seconds. Blood froze in his veins,
horror settled in his eyes, his mouth opened for a cry, a
scream.

Those knights and pages who of their own accord followed their young master to protect him, although no danger threatened in the middle of the solitary land, and who
now stood before the chapel, reins in their hands, heard a
cry, or a scream, and looked at each other. They exchanged
glances, and before they rushed inside with their swords half-
drawn, they saw Ulric in the door. He was leaning with his
elbow against the doorpost, his face white, his eyes confused
with unknown fear, his look hollow with deep terror. He
waved his hands and stopped the men with incomprehensible words. They wanted in, but their master, who had collected himself in the meantime, and to whom some clarity
returned into the eyes and speech, firmly ordered them to
return. They mounted their horses, and at a fast trot,
returned to the grove on the slope rising at the other end of
the gentle valley. Ulric stayed before the chapel. From the
other end of the valley, his men could see his figure moving
to and fro in the blinding sunlight, and finally, he bent down
and sat down before the door. He even waved away the page
who approached him bringing water and food. He spent the
whole night in the church, and his men wondered whether

– like James in Compostela to whom they were bound – he was fighting with an angel who would wound him in the leg and order him, wounded but purged, to return to the land of his forefathers, injured and victorious. Indeed, he came back in the morning, his body exhausted, but he told no one what had happened that night in the isolated chapel.

His face dark, without a trace of the former serenity, Ulric rode far away from his entourage, paying no attention to the farmers who greeted them or to the sunny landscape which surrounded them. He was silent; in the evenings he prayed. They spent nights in the open; in the nights his shadow was seen approaching the fires and vanishing into the darkness again. Even many days later, when they discerned the church domes and red rooftops of Amusca, Ulric did not rejoice like his entourage, who shouted merrily and spurred their horses on.

They arrived in Amusca at Easter, as can be read in Chapter 13 of the chronicle of the Castilian kings. *A great seigneur arrived here, the nephew of King Sigismund, Count of Cilli; he had come to the Kingdom to visit Santiago, accompanied by sixty cavaliers, all richly groomed noblemen. The King paid him great respect; he dined with him and sent him horses, mules and brocaded garments, but the Count accepted nothing; on the day when he left his country he had made a vow not to accept any present from any prince in the world. He took nothing. He was among the first to leave the great celebrations given in his honour by the King and the Queen for twenty days.* With the seal of an incomprehensible secret on his face the Count had been completely changed since the day and night spent in the chapel in the middle of a Castilian plain. *And so he left to complete his journey to Santiago*, as a chronicler of the Castilian kings finished his report. But, the report about the pilgrimage and the unusual event on the way does not finish here. It does not finish with a vow, gifts and long prayers in Santiago de Compostela, or with a long journey back. On the way back to the green, or by then perhaps snow-covered country from where they had come, they made a wide circle around the chapel, which stood alone opposite the forest on a slope, in the middle of an undulating plain. After everything that they had experienced at the Castilian court and in Compostela, they forgot about it, and some of the former gaiety returned to Ulric's shadowy face.

One of the pages from the entourage, who had stayed behind in Valencia to have a few horses shoed, tried to catch up with the rest of the pilgrims by taking a shortcut; in the evening he found himself quite near the place, near the tiny chapel on the red and white ridge in the wavy plain of Castile. Although he was tired and in a hurry, he could not restrain his curiosity. He forced open the locked door and entered, as Ulric once had, into the obscure nave traversed by the setting rays of the red Castilian sun. He looked around at the silhouettes of the saints on the altar and the indistinct images on the walls. Nothing attracted his attention. He was about to leave when, on the wall behind the baptismal font, he noticed the painted face of a bearded man who looked familiar. At that moment the red sunlight illuminated the entire picture, and the heart of the solitary visitor stopped: the severed head of John the Baptist in the hands of Herod, or whoever he was, bore the face of his master, Ulric of Cilli, whose tired bright eyes firmly stared at and through him. There was also the figure of a young woman, and for an instant he thought that he had recognised her face, too: it was the sad face of the unhappily fair Veronica of Desenice. But the page was not assured. It was Salome in the background of the painting, with a curious smile on the lips. Her dead white face with red cheeks could not have been Veronica's. It reminded one of hers, but the face was distant and dead. The page thought that it was his imagination that had brought this face into this shadowy room, perhaps the hot, red Castilian sun under which he had ridden all day. But Ulric's face attracted his horrified attention with great intensity. Ulric's face was definitely there; more than a month ago his master had stood at this very place and, surprised at first, and then more and more terrified, gazed at the strange image awaiting him just before the end of a long journey to an unknown country. How he must have looked at this mirror, into the features of his own face almost freshly painted, in lively colours! The garments on the body of the headless corpse were modest, of sackcloth, by no means those of a rich man; but the face, the nose, the lips still red on the severed head, even the colour of the hair and the thin beard – it was all there before him, irrevocably there! And then the page understood the scream they had heard, the cry of his master with dangerously penetrating, bright, somewhat tired eyes; the features of his master's face that he saw every day, the respected and beloved head, the loved and fear-inspiring head was now there, severed from the body, painted in vivid colours, red blood dripping from its neck.

For a short instant, which extended into long immobility, the page stood with a frightened heart, which suddenly started beating frantically before the incomprehensible image; then he ran through the door and gazed at the brilliant red globe of the setting Castilian sun, which hung above the undulating land, as if looking for an explanation for the mysterious and peculiar sight he had just seen, but was unable to understand.

A few months later – it was already dark autumn with the branches of naked trees projecting into the grey sky – the Spanish pilgrims were received at home with great honour and celebration. The pilgrimage was completed and the vow kept. The young count, who soon afterwards received the title of prince, was nicknamed "Spaniard", in memory of the successful journey to the distant country. The chroniclers wrote that in the following years he had good fortune on his side: he extended his properties, enjoyed the trust of European rulers, his wife bore him three children who ensured a brilliant future for the Cilli nobility. And when his brilliant luck was at its highest, suddenly the deepest fall occurred, bringing along the unforeseen ruin of the distinguished family. The children died one after another. Twenty-six years after the famous Spanish pilgrimage, Ulric of Cilli – at the height of his power, the commander of a mighty army, the last male descendant of a famous family before whom Hungarian rulers bowed their heads – was attacked by conspirators in the middle of the night at the confluence of the Danube and the Sava. He defended himself, fought back and, wounded in the leg like James to whom he had made a vow in Compostela, fell. Then he was killed and his head was severed from his body when he was probably still alive. Nobody knows whether the pious lord had time to say a prayer to his guardian from Compostela; nobody knows whether he remembered the image he had once seen in a Castilian painting in the middle of the bright silence of a hot day in a dark and cold chapel on top of a ridge in a foreign country.

The page, who also once stood before the strange painting in a chapel near Valencia or perhaps near a place called Sergoba, and who thought that Ulric's likeness in an ancient mural might have been painted by the red Castilian sky, knew that at the other end of the world a story was completed which had begun long before, in an obscure chapel in the middle of a Spanish plain. Or even before, even before the chapel was built and painted, in some incomprehensible time before, which the human mind has no way of comprehending.

Translated by Lili Potpara

Death at Mary of the Snows

In the great and terrible year of 1918, a young doctor, Aleksei Valislyevich Turbin, almost lost his life simply because he had forgotten to remove an officer's cockade from his fur hat. Mikhail Bulgakov depicts the event somewhere in his novel *The White Guard*. *There exists a force, which sometimes tempts us to look over the edge of a precipice, which lures us down into the emptiness*, the writer says. And so his hero Turbin, with a cockade, a lethal sign on his forehead, takes ten steps too many into Vladimirova Street instead of up Alekseyev Hill. At that moment, greyish people in army coats descend towards him from Kreshchatik, which is enveloped in distant, frosty mist. The young doctor is struck by the mad idea of playing a peace-loving citizen. But on the face of the soldier standing in front of him, there first appears an expression of astonishment, and a moment later of incomprehensible, menacing mirth. *The devil*, he shouts to the other, who comes running and pulls the breech. *Look, an officer*. Turbin understands nothing, but immediately turns into prey with wolfish instincts. A horrible pursuit begins. The entire street is shouting and encouraging the pursuers to kill the *officer*. Turbin shoots one of the chasers, but the pursuit does not stop. He is hit by a bullet.

Finally he is out of breath and hope. He keeps the last bullet for himself. He wants to shoot himself. *Nothing more could happen... And then he saw her, as if in a miracle, by a black, moss-covered wall*. When there is no more hope, when he wants to put an end to his life, the *Saviour*, as the writer calls the sudden female vision, hides him in her home. It seems that he would die of the bullet wound, but *the pain from his head slithers into her miraculous hands*. The wounded doctor and officer of the Tsarist army is secretly taken to his home, but his health worsens again. The wound is joined by typhoid fever. The doctor knows there is very little hope. *It was absolutely clear to everybody that this meant no hope at all*. Turbin is dying. But fate, which forces him to the edge of death, following its impenetrable logic, saves him for a third time. His sister Jelena lights a candle in front of an icon of the Mother of God and kneels before it.

The flame trembled. A long beam was like a chain elongated right to Jelena's eyes. Then her lost eyes distinctly saw that on the face, lined with golden beads, the lips moved and the eyes became so strange that her heart shrivelled with fear and intoxicating happiness. She let herself fall on the floor and remained motionless.

During the following days, Turbin manages to overcome the crisis. He awakens to life with a waxen face, deep wrinkles around the lips and serious eyes. The young officer of the Tsarist army was destined to die on the terrible run from his pursuers, he was facing death and he came back to life. Who once escapes death can never forget it. He or she remains marked with its shadow for life, with a waxen face and sombre eyes.

Twenty-seven years later, thousands and thousands of kilometres away, in a sequestered European nook which you cannot find on any serious map, a different life story is completed. In the great and terrible year of 1945, suddenly, following the unpredictable, and for the poor human mind, incomprehensible circumstances, the original situation is repeated. There is a Russian doctor, a former officer of the Tsarist army, in this case called Vladimir Semyonov, there is an approaching army in grey coats and there is the Mother of God. Vladimir Semyonov is marked by the death he once escaped. He is trying to hide from somebody, and is grateful to an ancient, miraculous rescue. A few years ago he built a chapel near his home and dedicated it to Her, in "eternal gratitude". With a hollow and insane look he searches for a

sign on her face. Is he asking for new mercy, a new salvation on his interminable run? Or, is he only trying to understand divine calculations according to which he had to be
saved once in order to find himself in the same hopeless situation so many years later? Possibly, the following true story
is imprinted on the life of Vladimir Semyonov for one and
only one reason: so that the playful will of fate could, in a
different place, a different time and among different people,
record it as a different version and a different way out of a
desperate situation.

In the spring of 1939, a stranger often comes to the villages by the Mura river. He attracts attention with his peculiar linguistic mixture of Russian, German and Slovene words.
Most frequently he stops at the chapel of Mary of the Snows,
and once, with few words, he tells the local priest that he is
a doctor. He makes inquiries about where to start a practice.
The priest suggests a larger town, but the stranger with a serious face, on which the priest, neither then nor later, can find
a single trace of a smile, answers that he is not interested in
towns. He would like to work in the country, and when the
priest jokingly remarks, "At the back of beyond, hidden from
God?", he gravely and sharply replies: "No place is hidden
from God." During the stranger's next visit, the priest cannot
but observe that he is very interested in the huge portrait of
Mary on the altar. With slight masculine embarrassment, quite
common in the region when discussing religious matters, the

priest tells him that Mary of the Snows received her name because a miracle happened during the construction of a church dedicated to Mary somewhere in Italy. The stranger listens to him carefully, a fact well remembered by the priest. He can no longer remember what year the miracle happened, but it was in August, and it suddenly started to snow. It is just a legend, the priest says, but the other shakes his head solemnly and maintains that a thing like this definitely happened.

Then he stays away all summer, but in autumn – some people believe at the end of September – a car arrives from Maribor, loaded with suitcases and carefully wrapped bundles. A fair-haired Russian doctor, in his forties, of delicate physique, by the name of Vladimir Semyonov, which soon becomes famous far and wide, starts general practice in a merchant's house. Before the year is over, the silent doctor is the most well-liked person in the area. Speechlessly, he touches wounds and bandages them. He inhales the odour of sweaty bodies, the stench of liquor and of sour wine coming from his patients' mouths. Without the irritated restlessness typical of physicians, he treats their fevers and fears. Whenever they talk of him, they soon run out of topics and words. They still know nothing of the serious man with a dark face. He can speak the language all right, but in his soft Slovene he rarely speaks more than is absolutely necessary. He does not attend the service, but is often seen before the altar dedicated to Mary of the Snows at solitary hours.

During the first few years, he frequently receives visitors from the town, among them a tall, beautiful woman. In the night, Russian talk drifts from behind the windows, which sometimes turns into rowing. Then the visits stop, and Vladimir Semyonov goes to town less and less frequently. The following years, he is alone more and more. In the years of 1936 or 1937, he buys a large factory building at an auction and puts various pieces of old furniture into it. He turns the ground floor into a consulting room. With extraordinary care, he starts treating diseases of the lungs and respiratory system. In the night a light burns in his windows, and he is often seen leaning on his balcony at dawn, silently watching the carriages stopping in his yard. Peasants with numb fingers arrange the blankets on their knees and wrap the sick into woollen plaids. The sick, with childish confidence, place their aches and pains into the hands of this curious man. Perhaps Vladimir Semyonov sees in their looks a mixture of humbleness and dark *muzhik* cunning; perhaps he notices their curiosity as they enter the house. But to all appearances, these people do not interest him. He meticulously deals with their problems, but not with them. He is interested in something else. He is interested in the news carried by newspapers, and more and more frequently a wireless screeches in his house. But before the rapidly approaching events take place, he does something which is soon known far and near.

In the winter of 1938, he saves the only son of a vineyard worker's widow from certain death. In these days and locality, pneumonia is a disease which rather certainly sends people to kingdom come, especially pneumonia in a vineyard worker's home. That winter, Vladimir Semyonov, for many nights, keeps vigil over the hallucinating boy. He sits by his bed, in a damp and cold cottage lined with clay, between dishes and cloths, together with the whimpering old woman. The recovered boy tries to kiss his hand – he can give nothing else as a token of gratitude. He presses his forehead, still shining with cold beads of sweat, into the physician's palms. The doctor pushes him away. He does not want thanks. The boy should thank her, Mary of the Snows; it was she who restored his health. And then he should thank his mother; she sat awake by his bed praying for him. These words bestow a saintly glory upon him. The village devotees spread the news around, and the story persists for decades after the events that follow.

And these events are approaching rapidly and inevitably. The same year the visits from the town are renewed. There are rumours that he is visited by Duchess Obolenskaya, the widow of Colonel Boris Aleksandrovich, the commander of the unit in Tsarskoe Selo. A number of times, Vladimir Semyonov is called on by a bizarre human creature in a long robe, with a dishevelled beard and long, greasy hair. He is called Fedyatin. The doctor's maid has it that the two stay awake all night, and that in the morning the room is filled with cigarette ends and empty bottles. Russian emigrants' visits from Maribor damage the doctor's reputation a little, but he is obviously not concerned about it. However, the visits again suddenly cease. It is unclear why the strange people stopped coming to that isolated place by the Mura. It is unclear what the night-long talks were about. What is clear is that Vladimir Semyonov is suddenly alone again, perhaps even more alone than ever before. And it seems that he wants it this way. He wants to be alone.

People gossip that he is afraid of something, that he has somebody or something after him, which takes away his sleep. The supposition gains ground when, in the spring of 1938, people notice that a chapel is being erected near the doctor's house. The chapel is dedicated to Her, the Saviour, in "eternal gratitude". Saviour from whom or what? It is becoming more and more obvious that Vladimir Semyonov did not choose to live in this area for the fresh air. He chose this nook to hide. However, soon after the chapel is completed, interest in the Russian doctor recedes.

On 25th March, Hitler annexes Austria to the Reich, and German uniforms appear on the other side of the Mura. Even these isolated villages are flooded by news and expectations. In April 1941, the Russian doctor constantly stands on his balcony, smoking cigarette after cigarette and watching the soldiers who are walking to and fro in his yard. A few days later the army retreats, and German troops come across the river, bringing German Socialism. Many people, especially the poor, greet them with pleasure.

On an October day, the doctor's house is searched and the radio taken away. The radio is returned when he takes two German policemen into the house. When they have a few drinks too many in the village inn, they question him about Russia and Bolsheviks. Vladimir Semyonov does not answer. From then on he locks himself in his room when he hears their nocturnal conversations. The policemen are often changed; in 1944, the last two are called to the front against the Russians.

In the summer of 1944, a patient tells Vladimir Semyonov that the Red Army is already in Hungary. Upon hearing the news, the doctor turns pale and quickly walks through the door. The winter is long, there is more and more illness, and Semyonov lives on black-market meat which the patients bring instead of payment. He hardly speaks to anybody. He often goes to Mary of the Snows; he is seen walking up there through the snow-covered fields. A candle is always burning in front of the chapel. One morning his maid finds him drunk, unshaven and with bloodshot eyes. He is sitting in an armchair with the wireless on.

And thus commences the great and terrible spring of 1945. The news that the Russians are in Austria passes from mouth to mouth. The Red Army is approaching the Mura,

the old Yugoslav-Austrian border. Huge crowds of Bolsheviks are approaching through the Hungarian plains. Roaring
can be heard from the distance. The house of Vladimir Semyonov is cold and neglected. He returns from his long walks
through the fields with muddy boots and goes to bed in
them. He speaks to no one. Now, a candle burns in his room,
too, before an icon of the Mother of God, before her pale
face, lined with golden beads. At night, Semyonov's motionless shadow stands on the balcony. Alone, he stands there,
listening to the roaring of guns, or perhaps to the stamping
of thousands of soldiers in grey coats. In May, hordes of dis-
banded soldiers wander around the village. Languages and
uniforms mingle. An officer shoots a soldier by the road:
theft or desertion. The corpse stirs a few times, and rolls
into the ditch. The end, it is again the end, and again they
are coming.

On 16th May, a village boy in a German uniform, bare-
headed and unarmed, comes running over the bridge. The
Red Army is only a few kilometres from the Mura; by the
evening, the first Russian regiments will reach the village. At
noon, Vladimir Semyonov orders his maid to scrub the mud
from the floor, clean the windows, wipe away the cobwebs
and dust. Then he goes to the neighbours' and commissions
mowers. For a while he watches them cutting the grass in
the meadow behind the house with wide strokes, leaving
light-green traces behind. The boys often put the scythes

down. They speak of the Russians, who are about to cross the river tonight. They look down the road. Everybody is excited; nobody feels like working. The doctor calmly encourages them to finish the work. In the evening, he comes out of the house, bringing wine for the tired mowers. He is clean-shaven, composed, wearing a bright suit. Suddenly he walks away, leaving them without the promised wages. Around eleven in the evening, the priest at Mary of the Snows is woken by a knock on the door. When he opens it, there is Vladimir Semyonov, with a pale face and dead serious eyes. He asks for permission to enter the church.

So Vladimir Semyonov is standing before the merciful face of Mary of the Snows, caressed by the flickering flames of the candle and the dark shadows between them. He is standing before the large and gentle figure which, in the cold of the church, silently, with little Jesus in the arms, looks somewhere past him into the darkness behind. This night, shadows dance over the tender features and the pink glow of her face. Semyonov does not kneel, he does not pray for mercy; Semyonov no longer believes that anything could stop the great and terrible army which has come after him, hundreds of thousands of soldiers, and the roaring accompanying them. He is looking into his past life, and asking her solely to help him comprehend this horrible misunderstanding. Images of the mad pursuit flash before his eyes. Images alone, not a single rational thought; there is no reply.

Perhaps he, like Turbin, with an officer's cockade – the lethal sign on his forehead – ran before the pursuers, their screams and shots. What dreadful act or what flight started all this in that remote year of 1918, that he was forced to run incessantly from town to town to finally settle here, where he erected a chapel to Her in "eternal gratitude" and kept coming to gaze into her merciful eyes? Which ice-cold river did he swim, in which damp cellar did he shiver while footsteps echoed outside, under which tree was he freezing, covered with snow, from which bloody ditch did he climb, whose bloodshot eyes did he feel on his back, whose murderous gasps? And so, in the cold, silent, tenebrous church, before Her face, resound the footsteps, shouts and shots, reflections of ancient fires and flashes of distant explosions. The stir of the harbour where he wanders for the whole of December of that even more horrible year of 1919. In a worn-out army coat, the young Russian doctor, officer of the defeated army, rambles through Odessa, thinking of his beloved who is far away, of his home which is no longer his. We can see him on 26th January 1919, boarding an old and decrepit French ship bearing the famous name of *Patras*. We can see him on a sorry piece of scrap iron, packed with despair and people with hollow eyes. With the collar pulled up, he watches the waves and surges of the rough winter sea, understanding nothing. Perhaps another member of the White Guard, Ivan Alekseyevich Bunin, is very near, imprinting on to his memory: *Suddenly I was completely awake, in a moment it dawned on me: Yes, this is it – I am on the Black Sea, on a foreign ship sailing God knows why to Istanbul, Russia is finished, and so is everything else, my past life is finished, even if another miracle happens and I do not drown in this malicious and icy sea...* We can see him in Istanbul, with the domes of Hagia Sophia in the background, which people dreamt about in the holy cities of Russia and, thinking of them, erected orthodox crosses. And true enough, the Tsarist army did come to the holy city, and Semyonov was with it; but he is only an insignificant part of the huge, confused, frightened crowd. Everything is terrible, and the world is coming to an end. But, he is alive, and twenty-five years old. He has left behind the face of death; before him are the cities of Bulgaria and Greece, the incense of Serbian churches, the suburbs of foreign, indifferent European capitals. Others are staying, they gather in groups, but Semyonov does not stop. Wherever they are, his brothers, there is also the breath of ruthless pursuers. When a turbulence in the whirl, which will, years later, scatter crowds of Russians around Europe, throws him into this region, he suddenly discovers this chapel in a European nook which cannot be found on any known map. To live again, without thinking of escape and return, never again to run or return anywhere. To live among these peasants, like a Tolstoy, to survive. Moments of fear and despair return when the emigrés come to visit him from the town, conversations, mother Russia, insane illusions; he is relieved when Fedyatin's Rasputin-like shadow disappears into the cold morning. There will be no more flight, no repetition of the terrible 1918 and even more terrible 1919. Naively, with all his heart, he trusts in the mercy bestowed upon him. When the roaring of the Red Army is heard from the distance, Semyonov for the first time senses the horror of a huge, absurd misunderstanding.

Time and space are falling apart. The shadows of the flickering candle flame are running over her face. Over her eyes, gazing into the darkness and across the river. The thousands of kilometres that he has travelled and the long years that he has survived: everything is disintegrating between the shadows. Suddenly, he is again exactly where he was once before. At the beginning, at the starting point. Twenty-seven years older and alone, he is standing in a cold church. He is looking for a sign in her eyes, to explain or help him understand. He feels icy cold in his chest and a deadly silence telling him that he is forsaken by Her and God, Her son, that there are no years behind him and no memories. With cold anxiety, he discerns the mysterious and somewhat ironic hand of fate, which did not bring him here to save him and put a full stop to his flight. It brought him here solely to record a different version of the story, which once had a happy ending. In the meantime, fate had been dozing, letting him live for twenty-seven years, and today, on 16 May

1945, began a new paragraph with the words: *It could have ended differently*. In that moment between life and death, everything could have been resolved differently.

The candles have burnt out, and in meagre morning light, Vladimir Semyonov still gazes at the immobile face of Mary of the Snows.

On 17 May 1945, at dawn, Vladimir Semyonov comes out of the church. His face is waxen and twisted with derangement. He stops on the hill among the crosses. Among the crosses on the hill at Mary of the Snows stands a Russian White Guardsman, looking over the landscape with empty eyes. Down there is the river and behind it a wide plain, gentle mist creeping over it. For a long time he cannot avert his eyes from the silent morning landscape across the river. There is no sound, no roaring. Everything is silent and hollow, like a deep, endless abyss. *There exists a force, which sometimes tempts us to look over the edge of a precipice, which lures us down into the emptiness*. An hour later, a girl meets him, carrying bright and clanging milk cans. The Russian doctor does not return the greeting, as if he could neither see nor hear her. Then he stands by the river, through the willows watching the fast and dark water.

His blind eyes awaken when he hears voices on the other bank. The roaring river becomes silent, the mist thinner, when he hears the voices of the two figures on the other side. They linger around in grey coats, rifles on their shoulders with fixed bayonets. The first steps to the water, and Vladimir Semyonov can distinctly and clearly see him as he speaks out: "*Posmotri, reka kakaja tjomnaja... mutnaja.*"

At first he feels something warm and familiar and gentle overcome him. He would like to go over there and hug them for having finally come. Then he sees the other one pick up a stone and throw it into the river. He can see him answer: "*Ona njet mutnaja. Ona takaja glubokaja... oãen tjomnaja potomu āto glubokaja.*" Now he finally realises that he has taken a step too many towards the abyss, and down, into nothingness. He sees nothing more; he can only hear himself ascending the hill, his loud panting and beating in the temples. His mad flight, which is frantically beginning again, or perhaps simply continuing, so that he no longer knows whether it is 1918 again or what, whether he is here or somewhere else. And then he suddenly stops. A sharp and clear thought cuts through him like a blade. He shall run no more; he shall haul no more hope along. He can travel another thousand kilometres and live another twenty-seven years. But just before the end, he will return to where everything began, in an empty and timeless moment between life and death.

Then he went upstairs and put a bullet through his temple. He had a steady officer's and doctor's hand, for the bullet only made a small hole and left behind a thick drip of blood which poured down his waxen face.

The Russian doctor, Vladimir Semyonov, was found

around eleven in the morning by the mowers who came to collect their promised wages. They laid him on the bed and crossed themselves. The young men respected the presence of death, but nevertheless they looked around for something to take as payment for the work done in good faith. As they fumbled around in their peasant awkwardness, they overturned and broke the framed old icon which stood on a cabinet. One of them took nothing. He was the boy who, with cold beads of sweat on his forehead, once tried to kiss the doctor's hand. And yet it was he who, unintentionally, with a dirty sole, stepped on the icon, on the golden beads above Her eyes.

People who liked the strange Russian doctor, despite all the love, later said that he had committed a great stupidity. And if stupidity was too harsh a word for death and such a sad end, then at least, according to them, he had committed an unbelievably pointless act. Everyone knew that the soldiers of the Red Army, in grey coats, never crossed the river. They stayed on the other bank. Everyone knew it but him. Let us forgive them these words, for our naive human mind is not driven by reason, but by infinite hope. And therefore, a simple human conclusion cannot take into account the possibility that everything was determined in advance, a long time ago, and that fate perhaps wanted exactly this denouement. We can complain about its cruel pranks, the irony and senselessness of its second version, but fate chose the ending. It left Semyonov to lie with warm blood pouring down his waxen face, and there is nothing we can do about it. It is common knowledge that this mysterious lady writes the literature which again and again places insoluble riddles before us. She can see beyond our vision. We can only see to the other side of the river, and not always, as this story proves.

Translated by Lili Potpara

Augsburg

I

Augsburg is a long way from here. I have never seen it. They say it has sixty thousand inhabitants and is very prosperous. Augsburg is the biggest city in Germany, and people like living there.

August. For three days I have been pacing my darkened flat. Outside, the August sun is shining. The radio is making great efforts to convince foreign tourists that Slovenia is a peaceful country. The war is somewhere else. The war is in that television set in the corner. In that hole in the world that keeps bringing me new corpses. In that box where the idiocies of propaganda alternate with pictures from a degenerate imagination. The speakers are mostly idiots. When the speakers are intelligent, they speak in square sentences. Everything is flat and lifeless. From political upheaval to change.

Upheaval? Change? Upheaval, yes, but what kind? Change, yes, but what kind?

The time is coming when I won't know how to rejoice.

We have had our fill of rejoicing; for two long years we've been carousing, and now we're waking up with a nasty hangover. Images from dreams are coming, images from the road. Bizarre pictures of our journey.

I had a dream about a chicken. It was being killed very slowly. Before we set out for Augsburg, we used to kill chickens. Kill chickens and debate aesthetics.

In one theatrical presentation in Ljubljana, actors on stage ritually slaughtered a chicken. They cut its throat and then a fair-haired actor held it by the feet. It jerked and flapped for a short time and then it died, since its blood had all run out, finally only dripping into a white basin. At that time, the young writer sitting in the theatre felt sick, though at that time he didn't believe in his sickness, which he took to be a weakness of his somewhat over-sensitive nature. He believed in Art and the Word, which are, as is generally known in the portrait of every artist as a young man, infinitely more important than blood or a momentary sickness. So he believed in Art, which maintained that the slaughtering of a chicken was "the poetics of sacrificial ritual", and in the Word, which added that the death of a white battery chicken was at the same time "the death of the literary, only aesthetically functional theatre in Slovenia".

That was long ago now, and the debate was still an aesthetic one.

When the Slovene youth theatre took its production of *Beauty and the Beast* to Belgrade, there was an incident. The debate was an ideological one.

The same artists incorporated the "politics of ritual slaughter" into another piece. A year previously, in the fairy-tale northern Austrian town of Prinzendorf the *Orgienmysterientheater* theatre of Herman Nitsch ("nitsch" in Slovene is nic, nothing, *nihil*) had killed cattle. Well, the Slovene artists killed chickens. And when in the course of the poetics of ritual sacrifice the chicken's blood began to flow, a well-known Belgrade dramatist flew into a total rage. Possibly he simply felt sick, like a certain young writer in the days when around poetic slaughter there would develop an aesthetic debate. But it was no longer the time for mere sickness or for moral debate. *Now it was already something else*.

"Fascists!" shouted the writer, very much *engagé*, as he noisily left the auditorium. "Ugh, fascists! Death to fascism."

This was seven years ago, and the debate was ideological. Before we went to Augsburg, we used to have ideological debates, polemic between the nations. We were still killing chickens, some industrially, and some in the name of the poetics of sacrificial ritual.

Since then, at a dramatic moment on the way to Augsburg, we have cut down the barbed wire at the borders.

On my desk is a piece of barbed wire from the Austria–Hungary border. That was the whole point, after all, wasn't it? To have pieces of wire on our desks, not running through our fields.

In Budapest a one-time border guard is making the wire that helped him protect his country into tourist souvenirs. He says the wire is the original, although there's no proof. "But what about me?" he says. "Aren't I proof?"

In a Budapest street, I think it's called Bajcsy Zsiinski, you go through a dark passage into a courtyard enclosed all round with tall old house fronts. I have often dreamed of this courtyard. Somebody has come running in from the street, where they were shooting, looking desperately around for some entrance hall to hide in. But all the doors are closed and the walls, like those of a prison, reach up to the sky. This was in 1956.

Now in the courtyard there are big heaps of barbed wire. A machine is whining, an older man is chopping off pieces of wire, and a younger one is packing them in neat boxes. Both are working intently; it is a peaceful scene. The barbed wire from the Austrian–Hungarian border is a little souvenir for American and west European tourists. For some time there was a brisk trade, as in pieces of the Berlin Wall. Now sales have stopped. And while the younger man raises his hands in despair over the big, still uncut heaps of wire piled up all over the courtyard, the older one wipes his hands with a rag.

"Don't despair, son," he says. "If you ask me, we'll still be able to get rid of that lot at a good price, kilometres at a time, wholesale."

He's been around a long time, the father. And there's always been that sort of wire on the borders or around the camp. It's not clear what he was thinking then. Maybe they'll sell the wire somewhere else, export it. Maybe wholesale for home use, on some other border. Maybe there'll be more work for the Czech specialists in minefields between countries.

This is something that Solzhenitsyn knows, too. As far as I know, he is still in Vermont, incarcerated in his estate by a barbed-wire fence, surrounded with alarms and guards.

On the way to Augsburg, we have ceremonially and light-heartedly knocked down our walls.

I also have a little bit of the Berlin Wall. What souvenirs! There was a time when what people had on their shelves were Venetian gondolas, miniature models, little gilded things and dolls that said, "Mama".

On the way to Augsburg, we've moved from upheavals to change, from dream to reality.

On the way to Augsburg, ethnic and religious wars have broken out. In ethnic and religious wars, the first things in line are pigs. On the way to Augsburg, we've been killing pigs. Some for food, some for entertainment. About the poetics of ritual sacrifice, nothing more has been said by anyone. Nor of the symbolic aura of the act.

A man who had survived the siege of Vukovar said that day after day through the cellar window they would watch an enormous pig that used to come to the square.

The people were either dead and lying in the streets or they were alive and cowering in cellars. But the animals had no sense and wandered through the streets and among the corpses, exposing themselves to the shells. This pig, though, had some sense. It didn't just wander about; it picked its way carefully across the square. As time passed, they noticed that shells never fell when this cool customer of a pig was in the square. Whether it was guided by some higher foresight or some animal awareness incomprehensible to man, the thing was in any case remarkable, and they gradually got so accustomed to the pig that they missed it when it hadn't been around all day. But there were many days and they were long, sometimes even longer than the nights. Then the food ran out, and they decided to eat the pig. The task was not an easy one. Not only did they have no food in the cellar, but no munitions either. The attackers fired with bits of barbed wire which mostly did not kill but left many wounded, so that afterwards, survivors said, they pulled that wire out of their heads in the military hospital in Belgrade. And so one day they spent the whole afternoon in total silence shooting bits of barbed wire at the pig. The shells, obviously, weren't falling at the time, and they were able to devote themselves to the hunt. The pig had a thick skin, since it had been well fed, and every hit buried itself in its fat. Sometimes, of course, it jumped and ran away, but it still kept on coming back to the square in front of the cellar window. Finally they got it in the head, and the same instant some shells fell on the roofs of the houses around. They made a lasso, and with it they tried to pull the pig inside. This even gave rise to some laughter, for the man with the lasso couldn't manage to get the twitching pig. Then somebody plucked up courage and ran under fire into the square, tied a sling around the neck of the enormous pig, and they managed with difficulty to haul the pig through the window. That's what happened to an animal in Vukovar.

This gave them a piece of theatre which shortened the desperately long time between attacks, between the explosion of the shells that left heaps of dead bodies. On the streets. Buried under rubble. Nobody protested.

And the chickens, asks the reader; where are the chickens now in this story?

They've gone; they were killed and eaten long ago, shortly after the beginning.

To Augsburg, we must journey to Augsburg.

We waited for a long time for one of our Belgrade colleagues to protest against the fascistoid treatment of animals. The pig that was done to death was not the only one. Many of them lost their lives in some such unanimal fashion, horses and cows, too. But nobody protested. Although somebody could have. They could have cited the World Declaration on Animals. Article 10: *No animal shall be used by man for entertainment or presentation not consonant with the dignity of the animal.* Nor did anybody say anything more about fascism. Nor, as far as is known, anything at all, which was perhaps even more sensible.

As far as is known, protests against the killing of animals during the siege of Vukovar came only from Vienna. At that time, somewhere in Slavonia, without any reason or purpose, most likely for the sake of "the poetics of ritual sacrifice", the so-called Chetniks killed a herd of Lippizaners. A high-circulation Vienna newspaper lost patience on its front page. "This Is Going Too Far!" it printed in big letters. Iranians in yellow nightshirts went through the cars with bundles of newspapers in their hands shouting: "This is going too far!"

On the way to Augsburg, we decided to build a new town.

Now another writer came on the scene, a world-famous writer, a professor, a Byzantinologist. At the time when Serbian forces were liberating the ruins of the Croatian town, marching into it with the death's head on their black flag, at the time when this splendid spectacle, with the liberators singing, "Give us salad, we've got the meat, we'll have Croats to eat", when this triumphant spectacle was being immortalised by Belgrade television cameras, and thereby winning the American Television Association's prize for documentary of the year, the voice of the world-famous writer and distinguished Byzantinologist was heard. This town, he said, must now be totally demolished and then completely rebuilt. It must be rebuilt in the Byzantine style. And at once everything became clear; of course, the important thing there is literature; drama, the literary vision...

They have told us that Augsburg is a place of peace and prosperity. Around it rage religious wars; bands of men with different new flags trample the fields, kill, plunder and rape. In Augsburg, however, people live and die consistently with their Augsburgian nature; that is, they also love, work, trade and vote their representatives on to the city council. Above Augsburg there are golden cupolas, the churches have baroque and Gothic altars. In Augsburg they have a richly furnished market and a repertory theatre.

Now we are nearer we can see: revolutions and changes are happening all around, from upheavals to changes. Everywhere new pictures. On the way to Augsburg, we stop in Buenos Aires. A lady in Argentina says it's the work of the Freemasons. All the communists who still weren't Freemasons have joined secret lodges. We stop in the Third Rome, too. A Russian lady professor from Moscow says it's the Jews, it's the work of the Jews. They used to do their work under communism from inside, now they do it under the cloak of "Catholicism". She has seen pictures of murdered Serbian children. They had stab-wounds on their shoulders and in particular places on their bodies. Jews, Freemasons and the Vatican, especially the Vatican. A degree of madness is sweeping the continent.

On the way to Augsburg, we are everywhere accompanied by new pictures. Dream images. Renewal. Of course, there was an upheaval, we can see that clearly; of course, there was. Now come the changes. On our way to Augsburg, we cross Slavonia. It is night. The train rattles through the still night. There is a rumbling in the distance. The fields are burned; dead bodies are floating in the Saya. A lone guard follows us with his eyes, his pupils red. Reality is changing, dreams are changing into reality. We are accompanied by bizarre stories. Along the river floats a bloated pig. A chicken flaps above it like some heavenly bird. In Budapest there is an alchemist's workshop. In Belgrade, in a big factory hall, a dark mass of people undulates and moves. A Byzantinologist with the skull and crossbones strides across the plain. To Bosnia! To Bosnia! A workshop in Hungary where they make souvenirs... the order will come soon for real barbed wire entanglements, the Czechs will receive orders for minefields, the Russians for concentration camps, the tourist industry will blossom on Goli Otok. Freedom, movement. Upheaval, change.

An anatomy theatre in Bosnia. And football. A literary historian playing football with a human skull... football is top favourite... a poet carrying a pistol... the poet is the commandant of a concentration camp.

Dear God, all this is true.

The excesses and obscurities of a Herman Nitsch in comparison with the images from Croatia yesterday and Bosnia today are just children's games.

Across Europe masses of refugees wander, and among them you hear the exhausted wheezing of lost animals. On the other side of the continent, millions of emigrants are preparing to set out for Augsburg.

But getting to Augsburg's not easy. We know that now.

On the way to Augsburg, I am still in my apartment, darkened for three days now. Outside, the August sun shines, and there is war on the TV. From upheaval to change... from change... to upheaval? Upheaval... change? Change, upheaval? In the Balkans, madness; Havel's state has split in two. In Poland there is confusion. In the "new federal lands", they are calling the former GDR, they are wandering through the labyrinths of the secret police.

Between dreams and waking come bizarre pictures. Dream images. Every day fresh corpses, every day more ruined houses. The fields burn. People with vacant eyes wander through empty streets. Severed limbs in a cellar hospital, holes in heads. The rumble of distant explosions. A glow over the mountains. What is all this? Something dreamed up by some devil, bored beyond endurance?

Augsburg. Augsburg.

Is it a dream? I saw an expert from some west European Ministry of the Interior sitting up all night long, the light burning above his desk, leafing through books all night long. One title could be read: Montaigne, *Journal de Voyage. The Way to Augsburg.* And another: Delumeau: *Fear in the West.* In the morning, when the feeble early sunlight blends with the electric light over his desk, he rubs his eyes, stretches and lights a cigarette. Of course there's a solution, of course there is – Augsburg.

So we find ourselves at the gates of Augsburg.

Travellers first find themselves facing an iron gate. It is opened by the guard from his room some hundred paces distant from the gate with an iron chain which "with twists and many turns" pulls out an iron bolt. When the traveller steps inside, the gate suddenly closes again. The visitor then crosses the bridge over the city moat and comes to a small place, where he shows his documents and gives the address where he will be staying in Augsburg. The first guard then rings a bell to warn a second, who operates the spring that is in a groove near his post. This spring first opens a barrier – also made of iron – and then acting on a big wheel raises the drawbridge, but so "that in these movements it is not possible to observe anything as they are worked through openings in the wall and gate and everything closes again with a great noise". On the far side of the drawbridge opens a huge door, wooden, but studded with thick iron. The stranger steps into a space where he suddenly finds himself in semi-darkness. But after a time another gate, like the first, leads him into the next space, where this time there is "a little light". In the middle of this space there is a metal cup hanging on a chain. In this cup he puts the money to pay for his entrance into the city. Another porter pulls up the chain, takes the money the visitor has deposited and checks the amount. If this does not correspond to the charge laid down, the porter leaves the guest to languish there until morning. If, however, he is satisfied with the amount, then he "opens for him in the same manner a further big gate, like the second", which in the same way closes as soon as he steps through it. And the stranger finds himself in the city.

One further important detail completes this, at the time, complicated and ingenious contrivance: under the spaces and the gates has been made "a great cellar, where there may lodge five hundred armed men, together with their horses, in readiness for any kind of surprise".

Now we are in Augsburg. In the year 1580.

When we have finished sleeping, we shall dream on.

Translated by Alasdair MacKinnon

A Sunday in Oberheim

Not even a Sunday, just a Sunday morning. Three scenes, a thousand words. And the necessary backdrop of the melancholy central European provinces. The square by the Danube: the river has risen a bit in the last few days, and the long-hulled boats, either on their own or with the aid of tugboats, struggle against the current, but they slide quickly and almost soundlessly in the other direction as the brown water foams. The wind stirs the tops of the poplars, clumps of white acacias toss in the breeze, somewhere up river it is raining, while here a dull and foggy light can be seen through the clouds. Organ music emanating from the church of St Egidio rolls over the cobblestones, and it bounces off the houses whose empty façades look like inside-out city walls; the powerful sounds chase each other and swirl around the Gothic building. It is deserted. Everyone is at mass.

Several cars park in front of the abandoned brewery on the other side of the tiny street on which I am living. I don't know why I've never noticed before. They park here, and some men carrying elegant gun cases in their hands get out and disappear through the broad door which must lead into a cellar or warehouse. Once upon a time, they rolled beer barrels here and loaded them on to carts. The brewery tower looks over the roof at the Danube. I'd like to be up on it, right on top. I'd be able to see where the misty rain from the low clouds meets the river in its upper reaches. Beneath the tower is a smaller, pretty well abandoned building.

"It was an ice shed," Fastl explains.

Fastl isn't at mass, ever. He doesn't want me to use the formal forms of address, just "you, Fastl". He once worked for the railway. Now he keeps a hot dog stand in the small train station. Jadranka from Bosnia cooks and sells the hot dogs. Every Sunday, when the stand is closed, Fastl goes to drink beer at the Black Eagle. You can find some others who don't go to mass there.

"They loaded ice with the beer," he explains.

"And what's in the brewery now?"

"Nothing. In 1945, just here near the entrance, three people were killed by a grenade from an American tank."

Another car parks in front of the brewery. A broad-shouldered man rings the bell by the door, waits and disappears inside.

"And where are those people going?"

"To the cellar."

"But you, Fastl, say there's nothing in the old brewery."

"Only in the cellar."

The small brown eyes in his big head shine puckishly.

He asks whether I'd like to see what is in the cellar.

"Yeah."

"Let's go," he says.

We cross the street. Fastl rings, and a man's voice can be heard through the intercom. They speak in a dialect I don't understand. The door opens and we find ourselves on a long stone staircase which leads down into the depths. It smells like sulphur and as if something is burning. I seem to hear a vigorous crackling, as if someone was smashing a heavy tree branch. Fastl walks cautiously, he is retired, and we are illuminated by the yellow rays of the cellar light. Down below is another door. My guide rings again and it opens as well. Now we're in a small room where a tall, close-cropped man sits at a table reading a newspaper. He nods, which means we can proceed, and we suddenly find ourselves in a bigger, better-lit room. It is full of close-cropped, broad-shouldered men, most of them wearing vests over shirts with rolled-up sleeves. Those same elegant gun cases are lying open on the table, and inside them are neatly arranged revolvers of various calibres, together with gun cleaning supplies.

"Shchutzverein," says Fastl, "a gun club." Some bigger

pieces are leaning against the wall – shotguns, Winchesters, some automatics. The crackling is now louder, the smell of sulphur sharper than it was upstairs. A greyish-blue cloud floats above our heads, and it hugs the high vaults of the cellar. There are no windows. The men walk out through heavy, metal-framed doors and come back in with serious faces. They handle their weapons like small animals, carefully and lightly, with practised motions. Fastl speaks with the broad-shouldered guy who just arrived. He nods. From underneath a bar covered with a forest of beer mugs, someone pulls out a kind of earphones and presses them into our hands. We go through the same doors, which emit a cloud of bluish smoke every time they open.

As soon as we walk through the door, we hear an explosion. A young man is holding something like a pistol, a Browning, a Luger, a kind of bazooka in his hands. Fastl and I put on the earphones; his eyes shine. Two people are shooting at a target with small-bore pistols; a young man with a bazooka is shooting at panels covered with human outlines. Some are closer, some farther away. They rise and fall, run as if scared, hide and rush out the other side of the hall. But the bullets from the spluttering gun catch up to them there as well. The walls are covered with thick foam rubber. The shooter is satisfied, though he doesn't say anything, wordlessly giving way to the next in line. He has a long barrel which he balances on his left elbow, aims and shoots.

Fastl points out to me that the shooter is hitting the target right on the head, in the forehead.

When we return to the first underground room, the broad-shouldered hippopotamus offers me a beer, and a close-cropped guy asks Fastl to ask me whether I'd like to try. I say no. The close-cropped hippo says that I'm no Heming-way, and I say that I'm not. The broad-shouldered guy asks whether I want a beer and I say no thanks. Fastl says that he will have a beer at the Black Eagle, just like he does every Sunday morning. Then the broad-shouldered guy and his close-cropped friend devote themselves to a discussion about the apparatus in fitness clubs, while Fastl and I climb through the yellow light up the stone steps. The greyish-blue smoke clings to us, and the crackling, as if someone is breaking up tree branches down below, gets farther away. It still smells of sulphur.

Outside it is Sunday morning. It is completely quiet in front of the scorched and empty bakery. The wind stirs the tops of the poplars; somewhere up river it is raining, while here a dull and foggy light can be seen through the clouds. The brewery tower looks over the roofs at the Danube. I'd like to be up on it, right on top. I'd be able to see where the drizzly rain from the low clouds meets the river in its upper reaches. I ask what is in the brewery tower. Fastl says, noth-ing, but if I'd like we can go see. I say no. The street is com-pletely quiet. "Nothing would indicate that people are shooting around here," I say. Lentia. The gun club is called Lentia. Fastl shrugs and cuts across the courtyard and the little garden plots on his way to the Black Eagle for a beer.

The main square is still deserted, and the organ in St Egidio has been joined by a powerful choir, whose slow *Te Deum*, as broad as the Danube, floats across the square and around the church. Around and around it swirls until it finds an outlet across the ground, across the cobblestones of the square, through the streets and over the roofs of Oberheim down to the brown water. I head down there together with the current of sound, to where a tour boat called the *Theodor Fontane* struggles against the river's current. Someone is standing by the railing and looking through binoculars at the town's façades, the poplars and the acacias from which clumps of white flowers hang.

A girl in blue jeans is sitting on a bench in the park by the river. Her shoulders tremble. She is crying. It is spring, the girls of Oberheim are crying. A boy stands next to her with his hands in his leather jacket. He is saying something to her, towards the current and then over it. They don't see me, though I pass close by.

Then I sit in my room and glance out at the brown waves that head toward the Black Sea. It is getting dark, the clouds have drawn nearer, beneath the windows someone is whistling, the light is no longer diffuse and translucent, it is almost opaque, then it disappears.

A Sunday in Oberheim

The radio announces that all the roads are blocked by Whitsuntide traffic. No one should travel unless absolutely necessary. I will write those thousand words, one or two more.

Translated by Andrew Wachtel

Ultima Creatura

Had Franc Rutar, on a humid afternoon long past, not fixed his gaze on the large letters of a book the woman sitting next to him was holding on her knees, everything would have ended much better. He would not have experienced the horrible things, which, even years later, when he thought of them with a mixture of painful discomfort and fear, appeared like images from some bad dreams. From moments between sleep and wakefulness. But he knew that this was not a dream, although everything had happened in a large, distant city, the pictures of which, just like dreams, were coming into his life from the TV screen. In the middle of a humid afternoon, he was rushing into the underground, and the God he met there was black and dreadful. At least, he claimed he was God, and Franc Rutar recognised him as such, although then and even now he thought he had been somebody else, God's dark antithesis. God does not think of such cheap tricks; he does not seek weak points in the weak moments of settled people in such a way. Franc Rutar was more and more certain of this, the more distant the unpleasant event became.

Sales representative Franc Rutar was a voracious reader. Although numbers and letters often danced before his tired eyes, he could not help swallowing every single word and letter that happened to be in his field of vision. He was one of those people who, in waiting rooms, in buses or just anywhere, read from newspapers and books that were not theirs. They cannot help glancing at the front page of the paper somebody else holds in their hands. Many do it out of laziness and tightness, some out of thievish impulses: they read over the owner's shoulder, and since they know very well how annoying this is, they always look away just before they are caught red-handed and start looking through the windows or at the tips of their shoes. Some of these readers never even think that they are actually stealing somebody else's property with their eyes, letter by letter, like bits of a female body, like bread from a table. Franc Rutar could not complain of a scarcity of his foreign trade and other reading material. However, reading the papers and books other people held in their hands became his uncontrollable passion. By doing it, he again and again tested his exact mind; Franc Rutar was a man with an exact mind and perfect memory. He immediately connected the dancing titles and fragments of pages into rounded logical wholes; a sports report was never mixed up with a political one. Anyone who has an orderly head can apprehend the order of the world, and mistakes cannot happen. His greatest pleasure was to catch a glimpse of a crossword puzzle; he could feel pins and needles at the sudden challenge and risk. He could test the speedy operation of his brain, which was one of his greatest assets in concluding risky editorial deals, rapid considerations, swift decisions. With brisk calculations, tossing the words around, he managed to solve the puzzles between two stops. Franc Rutar was of the opinion, according to his own beliefs, that he was one of the supreme achievements of the Creation.

On the very first day, he proved this fact to the colleague from his company with whom he had come to New York. After a few hours of his stay in the metropolis, he understood the mathematics of Manhattan streets, finding them no more difficult than the average crossword puzzle. Thanks to him, they were able to quickly carry out sophisticated foreign trade deals. On the third day, he felt at home in this human anthill of business, and he beamed at his friend's praise; that was the famous dexterity and ingenuity of Franc Rutar's mind; he did not lack reasons for satisfaction. Not even after he had, on the third afternoon of his stay – it was a stuffy afternoon, saturated with ocean humidity – appeased his hunger with cheap fried chicken in a fast-food restaurant. He contentedly sat on a subway train, which was to take him somewhere towards Battery Park, where he wanted to take a walk around Wall Street. He was in New York, his business settled, his stomach full, the world was high and life beautiful. But when the world is at its highest, the fall from the top is deepest.

He looked around him for an open newspaper. He was going to test his impeccable English in the risky game of connecting fragments into logical wholes, between two stops. He was about to get up to step behind the back of a man holding a folded paper in one hand and clutching on to the swaying handle with the other, when a better, for the moment of contentment more appropriate, opportunity arose. A beautiful coloured girl sat down next to him, actually a woman, a girl still, but a woman at the same time. She opened a book on her lap and was absorbed in reading. There was no need to stretch his neck, no need to stand behind somebody's back and look over a shoulder; luxurious reading was right there, immobile, open above the round, chocolate-brown knees. The letters were large, so he could easily follow the text written in simple English. The task was almost too simple. But he had just come from lunch; warm matter, mixed with fried Kentucky chicken, was lazily and happily flowing through his body. He abandoned himself to the large letters and the rocking train rushing into the black underground.

He suddenly felt excited and wide awake. The text resting on top of the naked chocolate knees, nicely cooled in the subway in the middle of a stuffy day above, was shocking. Franc Rutar had never read anything like it, at least not in a train: a young woman was just about to lie, half way through the left page of the book, with an older man, actually an old man, as it soon became clear. It was written in the first person, the narrator was the woman. She locked the door of her flat behind her; she was undoing the buttons on his shirt; at the beginning of the following page she leaned towards his neck and, with intoxicated desire, was smelling his aged skin.

Franc Rutar deeply resented any frivolity, temptations of the flesh, and contacts with strangers were in opposition to the order in his mind. He avoided all the things that some of his colleagues openly looked for on business trips. He once looked at the women in shop-windows in Hamburg, but to spend his hard-earned money on them never crossed his mind, not even in a dream. However, before the impulse reached his mind, he was all in a trembling frenzy he had never experienced before. Was it the humid day or was it the inconceivable fact that the young woman, who was not even a woman yet, was sitting next to him and reading such things? Also the sudden decision that he would not get off and finish the story in his mind, but that he would, on the contrary, actually read the thing on the knees, was spontaneous; it was not the product of consideration, but of some unknown impulse in his brain and body. Voraciously he read the next page, on which the senseless erotic scene continued, and he could only conclude that the girl in the book was either intoxicated, crazy or in love in some strange way. He waited impatiently for the slow reader to turn the page. He had long moments at his disposal to take a better look at her. He saw her moving lips. Moist, red lips. He missed his stop, but she still had not turned the page. She was moving her knees. A naive girl, he thought, she is embellishing her life with cheap romances in large type. She must work in one of those department stores, wrapping up clothes with awkward fingers all day long. He thought he would get off after all. At that moment, the round chocolate knees moved; she put one leg over the other, and turned the page at the same time. Everything happened simultaneously: for a long moment her hot thigh pressed against his with such strength that something rushed from his brain and his sex into his chest at the same time, whizzed towards his heart and there, above the top of his stomach, this hollow something settled down and refused to dissolve. The letters started twinkling before his eyes.

He did not get off. He heard the roaring of the train rushing somewhere into the underground.

She lifted the cover, and through the mist of his stunned eyes he saw on the fluorescent red cover the hollow between the woman's breasts, a broken necklace above them, crystal drops of sweat or water. The title of the book he read in a split second was: *The World Is Full of Married Men*. Whatever was holding a grip on his heart loosened, and what lay hollow on top of his stomach dissolved. He flinched, and his exact brain started working with computer speed, so that something cracked with fatigue a few times just under the arch of his skull. This here, he thought, this here is a set-up. This girl, his precise mind continued, is sitting on the subway just for this. The letters are so large so that somebody else can read them; under the book, chocolate knees. Yet, his mind crackled in an effort: Why? It is done differently for money. Because, his quick brain answered, because the girl wants to experience exactly this. She is coloured, discriminated against, frustrated. Where else can she find a businessman, an older man, even an aged man, if not on the subway? She might become his mistress; it is common knowledge that this kind of men in their most secret dreams want unpredictable events, young mulatto girls. At this conclusion, he again became pleased with himself, although not a bit less excited; if he had been merely excited a few minutes before, and before that only pleased, now he was both, excited and pleased. Excited flesh, contented mind. She had sat down next to him, not somebody else. It was true that his belly was growing and that he had a monkish tonsure on his head, although it was not showing. He must still have been immensely more interesting than the old man described with such passion on the strange pages of the book resting on the knees. I'll get off, he decided, where she gets off, and let happen what must. One can, after all, take a ride back the very next moment. He was astonished by such a brisk decision. If she asks for money, he thought, and prolonged the thought into a consideration, I can think about that on the spot. He was pleased with himself; the decision originated from his reason and contentment, partly from excitement.

The train was at that moment scurrying towards Brooklyn. We're travelling under the water, he thought, what an adventure, up there is the huge, dark mass of the bridge we know from films; he, Franc Rutar, is riding underneath it, a coloured girl is seducing him. He was looking at her knees, the rim of her skirt above them, he was touching her ribs under the light blouse with his elbow, his gaze fixed on her dark skin, he was travelling into her. Derma, his brain quickly said, five letters from a crossword puzzle. What's the matter with me, he thought, where am I going?

She stood up and smoothed her skirt. He stepped to the door, close behind her. He straightened his tie and thought it would soon be undone, just like the one on the pages of the book she was now clutching under her sweaty arm. On the platform she looked straight into his eyes; he felt the look penetrated deeply. No, there was no doubt about it. His heart was pounding. All he needed to do now was find the courage to address her. It would not happen without speaking. He was rapidly searching for words. He would speak in a muffled way, slightly through the nose, to conceal his Slovene accent. Her hips were swaying in front of his eyes; the light from the street approached and a house with a shabby façade above it.

He would speak loudly, so that she would not be able to hear the hammering of his heart. Before they reached the top, he had found the right words.

"Interesting book, isn't it?" he said.

"What?" she laughed with her pearl-white teeth. "What?"

"The book," he said through his nose, with a deep voice.

"Oh yes, the book," she said and laughed brightly. He youthfully jumped over a few steps; now they were in the street. Again he was at a loss for words in the empty space in his skull. He found them.

"May I buy you a coffee?" he said with an even deeper voice.

"I could buy you one," she said, so that he did not know whether it was an invitation or an ironic refusal.

If you came this far, the suddenly determined brain said, then go all the way. Or maybe it said nothing. The sales representative, Franc Rutar, probably because of everything unexpected that had happened in his life, was left without the brain which had helped him to conclude business transactions and solve crossword puzzles so successfully. If he had still had the brain, he would have seen that he was accompanying a young black woman at a fast pace along a horribly shabby New York street, jumping over heaps of rubbish and avoiding bodies lying on the sidewalks. Through black people sitting on steps, through their faces he pushed his way after her, after her all the time, through a door into a dark hall. From there new stairs led high up, between wooden walls close together. Through a narrow corridor, up the steep stairs he walked close behind her, with no eyes, with the smell of her derma in his nostrils, with his sweat pouring through his hair, dripping from his forehead and slithering into his shirt; with the smell of rotten wood which was covered in places with peeling wallpaper.

At the top she opened a door, then another. They were in a small room. Children's chatter was coming from the street, tenants' echoing calls from balconies and windows, and wild musical confusion from different directions. In the corner, in semi-darkness, stood a shabby couch with a metal spring sticking out. He loosened his tie, although he still expected her to do it before undoing the buttons on his shirt, as it was done in the book. Sweat was pouring from his face, his heart was pounding crazily, partly because of the run up the stairs. In a corner of his mind, not the one with swift and precise thoughts, but the one with a premonition, something said something; he could not discern what exactly it said. It did not run along the folds, it did not switch itself on, and even if it had, if he could have discerned what that something was which had said something, and what it had said, it would have been too late.

The dark girl sat on the couch in the dark part of the room; she looked emptily at the wall, opened her mouth and started screaming. Surprised, he looked at the disfigured face of the being sitting there, and he could not understand why, why she was sitting there screaming; he thought of somehow stopping that open mouth, from which a high, monotonous shriek was coming.

"Excuse me," he said, "this is a misunderstanding. I'm sorry." I'll hit her, he thought, why is she screaming, I haven't done anything to her, I'll hit her, he thought.

She did not scream long, towards the end not even very loudly. The door opened immediately. A young black man walked in, with a massive gold chain around his neck. He was chewing negligently.

"What's happening here?" he said. He mumbled the question rather indistinctly, and it must have meant what Franc Rutar had already understood: he was her protector.

"He wanted to rape me," the girl said, as she would have said It's four in the afternoon. The chewing man looked at him accusingly and with surprise.

"Who?" he asked.

She pointed at Franc Rutar with her finger: "Him."

At that moment his brain finally recognised what was coming from the vast premonition area. He was trapped. He thought he was a stupid, contented man, whose brain worked stupidly, following stupid instincts; suddenly he did not understand how he happened to be there at all.

"I'm," he said, "by chance..." It did not sound convincing. He was dripping with cold sweat, and he felt a strange emptiness spreading in his head, something completely unspecified, something like nothing. "I'm sorry," he said, "I'm sorry," and took a step towards the door.

The young black man pressed his back against it. It was impossible to leave just like that. If muggers stop you in the street, his memory whispered to him, have a ten-dollar bill ready in your pocket. Give it to them immediately, without wasting any words. He reached into his breast pocket and discovered with relief that the money was still there. Franc Rutar was a careful man, ready for anything, even for being stopped in the street by hooligans. But he was not in a street. He was in an unknown flat, in an unknown part of town, and the exit from this dive was blocked by a young man who was chewing and playing with the chain on his chest.

He never even looked at the banknote; he opened the door and called somebody. Immediately two other men walked in; they obviously could not have been very far away. One of them took over the post by the door; the other, a tall and slender middle-aged man, walked around the room. He was wearing a white linen jacket. He exchanged a few sentences with the girl, who was still sitting by the protruding spring; he spoke Spanish. He then turned to Franc Rutar, who with eyes full of hope was following his movements and speech. He said they would call the police.

"Yes," the sales representative whispered, "yes, the police."

Everybody went quiet, the young and the tall one exchanged a long look. "No," Franc Rutar said, "no need to call."

"Sir," the young man with the chain said, "Sir, your tie is undone." He lifted his chin and fastened his tie so tightly that he was left breathless. This doesn't make any sense, Franc Rutar thought, any sense. The tall man offered him a seat by the girl. He sank into himself and lowered his eyes. The tall man walked around the room and asked the girl questions; she answered with shrieking, bickering screams, the nauseating screech of the imagined girl with chocolate derma. The mumbling young man joined in the conversation, only the third one stood silently by the door. Oh my God, the sales rep thought, they are fighting for the prey. He was made to stand by the wall and raise his arms so that they were able to search him. Then he had to empty his pockets and, since there was no table, put everything on the floor. The young man with the chain suddenly became very angry. The wallet was not among the articles on the floor. He shouted something incomprehensible, he turned round as if dancing, and hit Franc Rutar on the neck with his half-open fist so hard that he instantly collapsed on the floor. At once he handed him his wallet. The white jacket asked him something. He did not understand, he did not know what to answer. He grabbed his hair and shook his poor head and breathed his sweet breath into him. He could not, he did not understand, he did not know what was happening.

"Oh my dear Mamma," he muttered to himself, "my dear Mummy, look what's happening to Franci." The girl opened his business case and emptied it on the couch. With clawing movements she scratched among his papers, put his pocket calculator and his glasses between the covers of the book; the tall one took the case. This is horrible, he thought, horrible what is happening to Franci far away from home; if his wife knew; he thought of everybody he loved who were so far away. But, what had happened so far was nothing in comparison with what followed.

He had to take his clothes off. He folded them on the couch. The third man, the one who was standing by the door without speaking, pulled a knife from his pocket, opened it, moved the blade down his neck. Then he lowered it to his sex. He'll cut it off, Franc Rutar realised, and put it in my mouth. The girl was frantically feeling his clothes. They were pushing him around the room and screaming over one another. Her shrieks were piercing his ears, the membrane of the tympanum, penetrating into the soft tissue of the brain. Somebody switched on the radio, somebody drank from a can, pouring beer all over him. The noise was terrible. Then for a moment there was silence in the room; through the veil of mist he saw a tall black man in a dark jacket approach. He came very close and quietly whispered into his ear, so that his head hollowly echoed with his breath and words.

"I'm your God," he said. "Do you understand?" Franci nodded. "Repeat," he said, "repeat: who am I?"

"God," he said, "my God."

"Your great God," the tall black man said, his head was just below the ceiling when he stood up; Franc Rutar was lying on the floor, the small head of the great God high above.

"My great God," he said loudly, as many times as he could. He heard his voice getting lost in the empty space, coming back with an echo, as if he had been speaking in a huge hall.

He was forced to lie on the floor and put his hands on his nape. They walked around the room and again talked loudly. They stumbled over him, somebody sat on top of him for a moment. Now... he thought... the knife. Or... a blow on the head. He could see his corpse floating under Brooklyn Bridge, the shadow of the giant bridge above, below, under the water, the rattling of the subway. He remembered he used to know a prayer. He started moving his trembling lips, pressed against the dirty wooden floor: "Our Father who art in Heaven." The clamour was far away, the musical chaos was coming from yards and balconies. Darkness fell over his eyes, voices and words, screams and slams of the door became intermingled. His body became insensitive, black shadows danced around him. He shrank into a little boy being put into a cauldron and danced around. Now they'll cut me into pieces, the dreaming boy in the bed thought, and they'll put me into that cauldron, into that big vessel Mamma used to cook jam in. Then he knew he was asleep, and that he saw his white body floating under the bridge, in its large shadow. The belly was slightly swollen, the tumult of the city coming from afar. The tumult changed into a shrill, hissing noise. Steam was hissing from a pipe. Again he heard Spanish words from a distance, then they became Latin; was it the tall black man in the white jacket speaking? He could hear two words quite distinctly; from a crossword puzzle, said his brain, which was obviously still working, from a difficult puzzle. *Ultima creatura*, he said. *Ultima creatura*. He rapidly placed the letters in the squares; his inner eye saw the squares and the two emerging words. Do these black gods speak Latin?

he thought with surprise; there is a certain logic in it, he thought, gods always speak Latin; is that what the black God is telling him?

For a long time he listened to the hissing of the steam, penetrating his awakening consciousness together with calls from the distance, from the street, probably from the balconies in the neighbouring buildings. He opened his eyes. It was dark in the room, a ray of light from the street fell at an angle on to his white body. In the empty flat – only then did he realise there was no glass in the windows – it smelt of humidity, decaying wallpaper, rotten wood. All his senses functioned: smell, sight, hearing, the aching body. There were holes in the floor, his clothes lay crumpled on it; in the corner a white, slovenly pile; the shirt, that was the shirt. The tie hung on the spring sticking from the pierced couch. He dressed. Feeling through the darkness, he descended the steep stairs of the empty house.

He arrived at his hotel towards morning. He told no one what had happened to Franci. To his friend who knocked on the door, he said he had been robbed in a park. He did not find it necessary to explain anything. When the friend looked at him with surprise through the half-open door, looked at the deep scar running from the ear towards the mouth, he closed the door and lay on the bed. Explain nothing. Say nothing. Even think nothing. He did not leave the room until he left for home. He lay on the bed and lovingly looked at the plane ticket and the passport, which had been, on advice from the homeland, left locked in the hotel safe. The representative Franc Rutar was a careful and sensible man. At least he still had a tiny reason for satisfaction.

For many years he dreamt he was being put into that big vessel Mamma used to cook jam in. He floated in the shadow of a huge bridge, with his belly white and swollen. In an empty room a black God leaned over him and breathed unknown horrible words into his ears. When the silhouette of an unknown city or bridge appeared on TV, he switched the set off and had a fight with his wife, who could not understand it. He always had it his way, he could not stand humiliation. He avoided young mulatto girls from department stores. Luckily, there were not many in his country. Never again did he read over somebody else's shoulder or tackle a crossword puzzle.

A few years after the trip to New York, on a winter night, by the fence of his suburban house, he knocked down a drunken tramp who had asked him for some change. "Creature," he shouted, "creature," and kicked the rasping heap on the ground. He was in the local paper, which discreetly published only his initials: F.R. That was all. Nothing else happened apart from the things that happen to anyone of us.

Translated by Lili Potpara

The Jump off the Liburnia

"Jump."

He was standing about a metre from the edge. The dark surface below was moving rapidly. He was standing about a metre from the edge of the ship's side, with one hand holding the rail at his back, looking at the water surface quickly moving past. His other hand swayed, and with it his slightly bent body.

"Jump," she said.

It was night, the shell of the sky closed by clouds above, the dark surface below. Perhaps it vibrated slightly; perhaps it moved along the sides of the ship like the back of a big animal. In the air there was the smell of smoke, which trailed from the wide muzzle of the funnel above them. There was no wind, but the smoke was nevertheless being pushed downwards, so that from time to time he felt its sharp smell in his nostrils, mixed with the fragrance of water, possibly of salt.

"Jump," she said, and her quiet, careless voice cut through the middle of his body and settled on top of his stomach. He could feel that something was actually drawing him down, into the depths. The feeling had emerged a moment before, maybe a minute before, a minute before he jumped over the rail and took a step away from her, towards the dark, rapidly moving abyss. A minute before he had been stretched on a deck chair, his feet by the edge of the rail; a minute before he had been smoking a cigarette. A minute before he had tossed the burning cigarette end over the rail, he had watched the flashing dot hang in the darkness for a moment, sway, and then draw a bright arc downwards. It seemed to him that he could hear a hiss on the surface. Of course, nothing hissed, nothing could be heard apart from the smooth hum of the ship's engine. It only disappeared; something, which a moment before had been in his hands, disappeared completely and finally, and after it disappeared, there was nothing left, neither in the air, nor in the water, nor in the darkness in which the ship was sunk. Into which they were both sunk, stretched in canvas deck chairs at the side of the ship, after dinner, without speaking, with vacant eyes staring into the darkness towards where the shore was supposed to be, where the shore actually was, since twinkling lights emerged there and disappeared again, on the shore, perhaps deep inland.

"Say it again," he said.

He tore his gaze from the lights on the shore and felt rather than saw the dark surface of the sea, the deep plane; his heart started beating faster. The feeling which lay on top of his stomach rose towards his heart, towards the hollow inside, towards the hammering in the middle of the body's hollow space, and the dangerous, frightened thought whizzed through his brain that he might actually jump; if she said it just once more, he would have no strength left to step back. She must feel it; this is not a game any more. If only a moment before, when he had followed the cigarette end with his eyes, when he had stood up and climbed over the metal rail, if it had all been a prank, then now, suddenly, everything was at stake. She must feel he is being drawn into the abyss; she must get up and hug him; she must at least be quiet. She was quiet. But it was not enough any more. Let her feel the fear running through him, for God's sake; let her be humiliated only for a moment; let her beg him, ask him to move. Why is she lying behind his back motionless, wrapped in a blanket? Why does she not, with a single gesture, put a stop to all the misunderstandings which have accumulated during the last few years in their lives? Let her utter just one word and the sudden madness will be cured, they will both be cured. He could feel that in this long moment she was probably thinking, judging his readiness for risk. It seemed to him that she had moved. She must get up, she must say a word, this will be a word of concern for him, a word of love and salvation. Let her at least say, you are behaving like a child; let her say, stop this nonsense; let her say, it's cold, let's go down into the cabin; let her say, the water is cold; let her make a joke, let her laugh, let her cough, let her yawn. He let go of the rail and his hands hung by his body, he bent his head. Where is the froth? Is it behind the ship? Where are the waves? Have they been swallowed up by the dark? He could feel her breathing behind his back, her eyes fixed on his nape. They were alone; a few young people were asleep in their sleeping bags, sheltered from the wind at the bow of the ship; no body could be seen, no hand or head stretched, withered corpses wrapped in silky textile. Say a single word, he thought, and you will be forgiven everything, I will be forgiven everything, everything we have done to each other in recent years; I'm sorry for everything, I'm really sorry, just say a word, he thought. This is not humiliation, or, is it humiliation if you take a step towards me, a single step? After so many years of marriage, after so many wounds, just a word; say, this is a silly provocation; say, one shouldn't play with things like this, shouldn't stand at the edge of the ship, shouldn't look down. Down into the intoxicating, crazily intoxicating depth which wants to draw one to it, flatten one on it, pull, sink to the dark bottom.

"Jump," she said.

My God, he thought, my God, now I'll really jump.

Actually, I'll just take a step forward, a step too many. Now I really feel dizzy, he thought. Now he can no longer think, what a horrible provocation, what has actually happened, why is he standing here being drawn over the edge? He cannot think of anything; everything has gone quiet – the ship and the engine, the beating of his heart in his chest and head – only the echo of the silence remains. He stepped to the very edge and swayed dangerously. I'm a good swimmer, he thought, nevertheless, at fifty I'm still a good swimmer; will the siren blow, will I be pulled under the ship? It seemed to him that she had got up. He desperately turned round; she had not got up. With the corner of his eye he caught the dishevelled head of a stranger, she poked it from the sleeping bag, the startled eyes of a girl. A mouse out of flour, he thought, and clung to the thought, a mouse out of flour; why do we say a mouse out of flour? How does a mouse look out of flour, what has a mouse looking out of flour to do with that dishevelled head, with the sleepy astonished unknown girl's eyes looking out of a sleeping bag? There's nothing I can say. I'll jump now, I'll step over the edge and a moment later it'll be all over. I can't do anything, I mustn't say anything, everything is hollow and quiet and crazily frightened, and yet decided. Say nothing.

"I'm saying it for the last time," he said, "say it for the last time."

Because of the gaze, transfixed by the dark running surface, the depth, because of the magnetism drawing him down, because of the something with no name, his body started trembling. What is it, he thought, am I drunk? They had drunk a bottle of wine over dinner. Will I swim out? I'm not drunk, I won't swim out. The thought was looking for an exit in fast, energetic thrusts. The sea is the Adriatic, the ship is the *Liburnia*, we are wife and husband, many years at the edge, now I'm standing at the edge, in the distance, on the shore, there is light, the depths are dark, the ship is wrapped in darkness. Sometimes, when he stood on the tower by the pool, on a rock by the sea, when the tiny boy's shuddering body, the frightened trembling soul, wanted to show his friends that he dared, that he really dared, he used to count, count to three, and then he always jumped: when he started counting he knew he would jump, although he knew there would be terrible moments of absence during the fall, that it might hurt down below, the impact on the surface. Now it was different, everything was the same, but nevertheless different. The point now was to spring into the heart, not into the sea, his heart and hers, the heart in which everything began and acquired its sense. But to accomplish this, she must utter a word, a single word; it must not be a humiliating word, it must not be the ironic: jump, it must not be: jump-because-of-me, it must not be his failure at this edge, this moment, can she not feel it in her chair, wrapped in a blanket, this moment life can start anew. This moment his body is trembling, can she not see it, this moment he is really irresistibly being drawn to the depths. The brief laughter of young people drifted from the deck, a door slammed, a discarded bottle rushed past in the sea, the dome of the cloudy sky lowered. He felt his palms were sweaty; beads of cold sweat emerged on his forehead, cold wind started blowing and again he could feel the stinking smoke from the ship in his nostrils. Will this be the end, the last sensory perceptions he will take over the edge, into the emptiness, into the dark? Or will she now say a word, another word?

"I'm saying it for the last time," he said, "say it for the last time." He said it twice, it was like counting to three in his boyhood years, he said it twice, at short intervals he answered quickly, angrily, challengingly, humiliatingly, now is three, a moment later I say three, I'm saying it for the last time, he said, say it for the last time.

"Jump," she said quietly.

She said it quietly, she said it with a quieter voice, and this stopped him for a moment. But at the same instant the thought caught up with the brain that she had said it, said it despite everything, she had said what she should not have said for anything in the world, and he sprang over the edge. Actually, he did not spring, he had no strength left for that. He simply took a step forward; he simply moved his foot and collapsed into the dark empty space. To tell the truth, he did not step into the deep void, he slipped into it. He sat at the edge, clutched the metal frame with his hands and slid along the edge towards the rapidly approaching, larger and larger, more and more painful surface of the sea.

No ground under the feet, nothing to hold on to, he flew through space, through the dissolved and supple airy matter. The cloudy dome of the sky and the blue-black surface of the sea were turned upside-down and merged. Now the sky was below, then it was carried away and blurred; now something gradually rose in his chest, then his heart was captured by its own trembling which at the same time was the trembling of the air through which he flew. Everything was visible and yet invisible, the direction of the fall was simultaneously up and down, the curve of the horizon was rounded, gravity was derailed, the unity of the world became denser and at the same time open, the water and the air, the sea and the sky. The bodily matter disintegrated on contact with the immobile surface of the sea. For a moment he could see the light on the shore towards which he was supposed to swim; for an instant he saw the immense shadow of the ship, its metal side, its dark body rushing past, dragging him towards it. He heard a scream, a shrill when he heard the roaring of the ship engines, their coughing and stopping, the grumbling signal siren; when he heard it all he was far behind, in the middle of the spuming waves the monster was leaving behind, far below without vision or hearing, without breathing or pain, enclosed in the watery matter, the disappearance, the prenumbness.

She was still lying wrapped in a blanket, now, by the white metal wall, in the dark. She lifted her head only slightly. The girl with the dishevelled hair and mousey, tiny, sleepy eyes lit a cigarette. She raised her head only slightly to see him more clearly clutching the metal rail, murmuring something into his chin. He did not swing himself over the edge, he did not move his foot and with a single step fall into the void, he did not slide along the side of the ship towards the rapidly approaching, larger and larger, more and more painful surface of the sea.

He did not jump. He did not spring into the centre, the heart, the place where everything began and acquired its sense. He did not throw himself anywhere. He stood by the rail and felt that his trembling body was calming down, that the hollow void in his head and chest was filling with noises, senses, looks. The ship alone was shuddering with the jolts of the engine, the sharp, stinking smoke was filling his nostrils; he looked towards the shore and watched the approaching lights of a town. I'll hit you, he thought, I'll kill you. Down in the cabin, if not here, then down in the cabin.

"How could you," he said, "how could you?"

A warm wind started blowing from the shore. The lights of the town were approaching. If he had turned he would have seen that, despite the warm wind from the shore, she had pulled the blanket up to her chin. If he had turned he would have seen there was nevertheless a hint of surprise and uncertainty in her eyes. Not fear, simply uncertainty and surprise. This would have sufficed. But he did not turn.

"What does *Liburnia* actually mean?" she said quietly.

He was silent. How could you, how could you?

"You don't know?" he said. "It was an ancient Illyrian kingdom. You don't know?"

"It's cold," she said after a while, "let's go down."

It was not cold, it was warm; warm wind blew from above the stony hills, with piles of stones on top, ancient Illyrian graves. There it probably roared and howled around the peaks, from there it blew clouds above the water, here it dissolved into a soft mass of air above the sea surface which was suddenly no longer an oily, quiet surface but a slightly wrinkled one, with frothy crests in places. The girl in the sleeping bag drew a few more puffs from the cigarette, then she threw the burning end over the rail, into the dark. The wind held it for a while, then forcibly carried it along the side of the ship, back and down. The dishevelled hair disappeared. She zipped up the sleeping bag over her head.

"Let's go down," he said. "Let's go now."

Translated by Lili Potpara

The Savannah

Scarce grass, antelopes, the sun, a fat snake rolled under a heated rock. At a sharp curve the bus climbs up from the plain on to the hill, rattling, shaking. The conductor, his unbuttoned shirt displaying a shock of curly hairs, is leaning over the back of a seat. Sunk into the seat, beneath his breathing, is a fair-haired girl. The girl is a "Miss": so she is addressed by the man leaning over her. Her knees are lifted high on the seat-rest before her; in her lap lies an open folder filled with drawings. Over the white surface the pencil draws a shaky line, the tip jumping off the paper. The line dances towards the edge, leaving no recognisable image.

"And what are you drawing?" asks the man. His skin gives off a strong, sweaty odour.

"Animals," says the girl, "antelopes, snakes. Stuff like that."

146

"Oh?" asks the conductor, looking at the unsteady, broken line on the white sheet. And at the lacy edge of the rounded knees. Just above them is the edge of a lace skirt like those worn by peasant women in Bela Krajina or the Ukraine and bought in the fancy shops of large cities; a linen skirt, and further down at the ankles, rolled-up socks. He is looking at the lace and the socks, feeling hot; the air in the vehicle is humid.

"But up there, in Kot," says the hot one, "there are no antelopes there." He laughs. They both laugh.

She laughs back: "There I draw windows... And those flowers hanging out," she adds after a while.

The man with the bag strapped over his shoulder stumbles through the heated bus among the workers and peasant women carrying baskets. He sways, the lace dancing before his eyes.

"Did you see that?" he says, throwing himself into the front seat, wiping his nape with a handkerchief. "Did you see the lace?"

The driver rocks in his seat and looks in the rear mirror above.

"Good lace," he replies.

And as their eyes meet, both burst into a short laugh.

The last stop is Kot; the bus turns in a small square in the middle of the village. The village is pressed against a hill; to the left and to the right, in a semi-circle, spread mountain clearings, yellow and white with spring flowers. A peasant is standing next to a tractor before a shop, sipping beer from the bottle. The young girl looks up into the incandescent globe of the sun, at the white sand in the village square, at a stone wall with a green lizard running over it.

In the dark, empty public house, the two men from the bus are sitting by the window. A huge fly is buzzing around, battering against the glass. The men are silently scooping up pieces of bread soaked in goulash. Their eyes wander pensively through the window, past the irritating fly, to the square, to the girl sitting on the wall. She is holding the folder on her knees, drawing lines along the sheet with different coloured pencils; she is holding a number of them between her teeth and at least two at a time between her fingers. Underneath the lace, underneath the rolled-up skirt, is a patch of sun-tanned skin, the lower part of a smooth, fleshy thigh. Then she stands up and walks across the hot, glittering square, looking towards the meadows in the distance; with supple, gentle steps she disappears among the houses.

When, in the afternoon, the bus from Ljubljana again returns, the shadow of the church belfry is falling across the square. In front of the shop, tractors are standing, and peasants nursing their beers. There are loud voices and there is laughter. She is sitting on one of the tractors, a bottle of beer in her hand and drawings and pencils in the loose skirt. She is telling them something, a man cries out, and all laugh in a loud voice. Then she slides off the tractor, somebody helps her down and, as she lands on the ground, the papers from the folder scatter around. She picks them up, arranges them neatly, and puts the folder under her arm; with soft sandalled tread, she heads for the public house. Two men take a few steps after her, and the dog behind the fence barks, pulling itself off the chain.

"A lion," says somebody from the crowd, "a tiger."

They laugh, then climb on to their tractors, start the engines and head for different directions, towards the yellow grassland and up the dark-green hill. It is still hot, dust is whirling from under the wheels; the dog goes on barking until the girl with the drawings disappears in the pub's hall, then it curls up in the shade by the fence, howls a few times, and is suddenly asleep, as if it had dropped dead.

Inside, in the cool, slightly dark room, the two from the bus are sitting by the small window. Their heads are sunk between their shoulder like lizards' between their scales; watchfully, they follow the girl's movements. She contemplates the pictures on the walls, sits down by the earthen stove, places the folder on the bench beside her, pulls her legs up to her chin, joins her hands below the knees, looks before her. Would she like a drink? asks the one with the bag, pulling his head, lizard-like, from between his shoulders. Yes, she nods – wine; the waitress brings the wine, she takes a sip and smiles.

"Thank you," she says, "we already know each other." The men exchange glances. The lizard pokes out his head and walks across the room to her: could he see what she has drawn? An antelope? She wiggles her forefinger, motioning him to lean down to her, to the freckled nose and strangely glimmering eyes; he breathes in the fragrant smell of her skin, almost touches her fair hair, beads of perspiration flickering between the thin hair on his forehead. She whispers something.

"I don't understand," says the man with the unbuttoned shirt.

"I've drawn a pig," says Miss, loudly, "you, the pig."

The man steps back, quickly, as if slapped, straightens up his torso, pulls the head between the shoulders. He hastily readjusts the bag so that something jingles within. He looks at his watch.

"Let's go," he says to the other one, still seated by the table. "Time to roll."

"Did you see that?" he says afterwards, when they sit down in the hot, half-empty bus going from Kot to the town. "Did you see the slut?"

"Doesn't matter," says the driver.

"It does matter."

Then it is night, and time for the last journey. They walk out of the pub, leaving behind the noisy farmers by the bar; the night is moonless, no passengers are waiting. But, as they get on the bus and switch on the light, the girl in the lacy skirt is sitting in the back seat. The driver starts the engine; as it is warming up, rattling, the conductor with the bag slowly rocks down the aisle towards her. The light is out, a dark shadow is crawling in. He grabs the seat-rest with both hands and leans down to her knees.

He looks into her bright eyes; her gaze is fixed on the window, into the darkness beyond.

"A ticket," she says, without looking up.

"You don't need one," he says, "it's all right."

The heavy vehicle roars and sets off. The man with the bag sways off to the front. She remains in the dark. Voices penetrate from outside, screaming vultures, those with hooked beaks, ravens, and the pained howling of a hyena.

"Stop," says the man with the bag.

"Don't be stupid," says the driver.

"Stop, I'm telling you."

The brakes screech, the bus stops on the country road. It is dark, no light anywhere. The paw-like rocking steps proceed slowly down the aisle, a kind of gasping breathing. Then he is beside her. His head is sunk between the shoulders; he pulls it out slowly, stretching the skin on the neck and down the back.

"I have more wine," he says.

"No," she says. "Don't want no more wine."

He sits down next to her, puts one arm round her

shoulders, pulls her towards him, shoving the neck of the bottle into her face.

"Oh yes" he says, "you'll drink some more."

He takes a swig, and when her body twitches in an effort to pull away, he claws his fingers into her hair, searching her mouth with the bottle. The other stands in the aisle looking into the darkness, listening to the growling and pushing at the back. Then, a scream stopped by a sweaty palm. The bottle falls on the floor, shatters with a hollow noise, the air is instantly filled with the smell of wine, of sweat.

"Damn it," he says, "I've cut myself." The smell of blood. "Stop staring," he says into the darkness, "help!" The other walks down, reaches between the bodies, grabs the cloth, tears the lacy skirt.

"I can't," he says. "What do you want me to do?" A blunt slap lands on her face. Her body is suddenly calm, the hands feel some coagulated mucus on the belly, an animal is pacing around.

Then she hears the buzzing of insects, a shiny, red-rimmed globe is high in the sky. There are no flowers in the plain where she lies, only shocks of dry grass and thorny shrubs. Far behind in the savannah is the silhouette of the belfry and the church in Kot. The hooves of a herd of antelopes stamp across the hard soil and disappear in the distance raising a cloud of dust. A lizard with yellowish skin, with a scaly, horny shell is creeping through the thorns towards her hand. And a fat snake, curled up under an incandescent rock, very slowly stirs.

Translated by Lili Potpara

The Look of an Angel

Above the tops of the Pohorje pines, the wind is howling like an unhappy and lonely wolf. At unequal intervals it moves away, and somewhere in the valley it roars as if its invisible mass were hitting an invisible barrier. Then it comes back and whirls the clouds of snow among the trees, so that the trunks around the clearing screech and whine. The look of an angel rapidly moves down, pauses on the bent tops of the pines, like a blade cuts through the air, and a moment later through the dark crown, among the branches, down the crusted trunk. Below, there is less snow, more darkness and silence, interrupted by whining wood, its taut tissue and roots fixed in the ground like claws. Now it runs above the ground briskly shunning the black bodies of the trees, then rises above the snow-covered bushes at the edge of the clearing. The wind is dragging behind a snowy mist over the sloping open space. Above it the field of vision extends; at the other side it is limited by the slope of a high hill disappearing into the cloudy zone on top. A wooden house is pressed against the foot of the ridge, window-deep in snow, to the left is another building, no path anywhere. Under the projecting roof, two people are standing, wrapped in sheepskins. The smaller one is a woman, the stout one a man; they are standing immobile under the roof, looking into the pathlessness before the house. Behind, the wind howls like a wolf on the ridgy slope, wails into the valley where it roars, sending back the roaring echo. The woman looks up, following the bellowing of the snowstorm. The man stirs, waves his hand, leans down, looks at her questioningly, glued with white eyeballs and tiny pupils to her white face; the woman shakes her head. The stout man draws himself up, and again they stand motionless. In this immobility she once again moves her head, shakes it. The eye at the edge of the forest quietly watches them. Then it moves, silently it approaches across the inclined clearing, in a sharp straight line through the blizzard directly towards them; a few steps away it stops, listens to the beating of their hearts, the warm flowing of their blood, fast breathing. Then it rises and moves up, past the man's tanned, wide face, his small, incessantly winking eyes with crusted brows and lids, towards her; it observes the blotches on her young white face, lips turned blue; with its look it touches the thin blue vein pulsating on her temple.

Through the gap of the half-open door, it slides into the dark hall and further in. Into a low chamber, where a glimmering candle is palpating the murky corners. Where an old man is lying on a bed. Bony hands on the blanket reaching up to his neck, wrinkled pale face, beads of perspiration on his forehead. His eyes are closed, he is breathing feebly, and he whines in a low voice. The flame of the candle twinkles, shadows dance across his face, and he quickly opens his eyes.

"Anica," he says quietly, "Anica."

With a shaky hand he reaches for a cup on the chair by the bed; he tries to pull himself up on the elbow, overturns the cup; the liquid pours over the rim and starts slowly dripping onto the uneven wooden floor. He falls back on the bed and calls her name with all his might, the name of Anica, who cannot hear, who is standing with a stout man under the roof, listening to the wailing of the wind. The eye lurks motionless in the dark corner, under the crucifix. The old man is moving his lips, silently forming words. He slowly turns on to his hip, breathes heavily, and sees the candlelight flicker quickly around the room. By the door somebody is shaking snow off the shoes. The woman walks in with the fur in her hand. She stops by the bed and looks at him. She stands for a long time, letting the time pass. The old man moves his body, and again he is lying on his back with his eyes fixed on the ceiling.

"Who were you with?" he asks.

"Who was I supposed to be with?" she asks.

"With Cretin," says the old man.

"Cretin is in the stable," says Anica.

"Good," says the old man; "he can't come into the house."

Anica steps to the bed, arranges his pillow, offers him her warm elbow, and his cold fingers close around it. He is looking at her face, his eyes are tired, they are looking at her face with hope. Her face looks weary, her eyes vacantly gaze ahead, just as they watched the whirling of the snow on the clearing in front of the house. The thin blue vein on her temple is not pulsating any more. The eye moves from under the crucifix to the bed; it lowers itself between their faces, between both looks, between the tired and the vacant.

"Somebody is here," the old man says.

"Who could it be?" says Anica. "No one's here."

The look slides through the narrow slit of his eyelids, into the tiny pupils and red bulbs around them. The eye is now looking out of the old man, with his eyes; it takes over his sight.

"Jesus," the old man says, "it hurts behind my forehead."

Through the red mist, the eye can see a woman's hand moving closer. It is blue with cold; her cold and rough skin touches the forehead, presses, stops. It rests there for a long time, the eyes close, weakness in the body, feeble heart beats peck at the dome of the skull. Her cold hand, warm elbow above it, her young body, from which vital juices are flowing into him, invisible juices, which have been flowing out of his body, mercilessly and invisibly all these days since he lay down. The hand moves away, he opens his eyes again, the room still looks misty red, the flame of the candle is quietly flickering. Her back, leaning towards the bed, cleaning the spilt liquid. Then her invisible movements around the room, some objects she is bringing to the bed and placing on the chair beside it. A rattle by the stove, she is putting wood on the fire, metal sounds. Then she sits for a long time, looking ahead of her, at the floor. Now he can discern familiar movements, the sound of the hair being undone, and then the slow, patient combing.

"I know who you are combing your hair for," the old man suddenly says and pulls himself up on his elbows, so that the room in front of him sways in every direction. "For him, for Cretin." The heart beats are faster, although still weak. She does not answer; again she slowly fastens her hair. She turns her head towards him; he cannot see her eyes; her face is wrapped in a red mist. The wind shakes the house a few times, wails, howls, blows up the slope of the hill, disappears.

"I'll take your blood," she says quietly, gets up. His eyes close, he listens to her steps moving away, to the hall, then back to the bed. He opens his eyes and follows the cracked vessel she places on the chair. She is undoing his buttons; her hand opens the shirt on his chest, the other is taking little animals from the vessel and pressing them on to his skin.

The leeches wiggle between her fingers, changing into cold, slimy, slightly rough touches.

"You will sleep now," she says.

"I don't want to sleep," says the old man. "When I sleep, nightmares come. Nightmares," he says, "nightmares are souls, which leave sleeping people and go scaring others in their sleep."

The look runs out from the narrow slit of the old man's half-open lids, out into the misty red light, which immediately dissolves. It rises slowly to the ceiling, and from there watches the work with the leeches.

"You always say that before you fall asleep."

The eye is looking at her from the ceiling. She stands by the bed for a long time, waiting for him to sink into sleep. Feeble strength is flowing out of his body, his eyelids are closing; every now and then they open and reveal the white of the eyeballs.

"The bad blood will come out," Anica says. She is still standing by his side, until his lids close and only a sunken, tight wrinkle remains instead of eyes. She pours some water into a vessel, puts it on the stove to heat and slowly undresses in the meantime. With lips pressed tightly together she looks at her body, slightly drooping breasts, red streaks on the skin impressed by the rough clothes and ribbons. She puts the vessel on the floor; before she squats over it, she looks towards the window a few times. Her lips are moving in an unknown dialogue; she is looking towards the window and around the room. The old man whimpers in his sleep, moans like the trees down by the roots, bent in the wind. Her hands reach for the hot water, scoop it, take it to her pubic region. She washes herself slowly and composedly, her lips still moving. Her look drifts to the crucifix in the corner, rests on it for a few moments, God sees everything, God knows everything. In the church, down in Sveti Lovrenc, a big, shiny God's eye is painted on the wall above the altar. Now it is in the darkness of the cold church; all the paths leading to it are covered in deep snow. She knows it, yet she shivers and, frightened, looks towards the small windows. She stands up quickly, with skilful movements dries herself, pulls up her underwear and sits on the bed. She kills the candle with her fingers. She listens to the wailing of the wind, which does not cease, to the now feeble and even breathing of the old man. The eye is resting on her, it has moved into her, the look gazes from inside her into the darkness; together with her it is waiting for something that must happen. She can hear roaring, outside it is roaring like the sea she has never seen. A frail light sparks behind the window. Anica stands up and quickly throws the fur over her shoulders. She quietly opens the door and tiptoes through the hall. The stout man is standing under the projecting roof, with an oil lamp in his hand. Behind his back the singing wind is blowing dancing snow flakes in the glimmer of the trembling light.

"He's asleep," Anica says. The man turns round, and walks through the wind and snow back towards the stable. After a few steps he turns round. She is still standing on the threshold.

"So?" he says. She looks back into the dark hall, then moves away from the door and quickly walks after him. The look steps out of her and follows them through the sea of the roaring wind. They sit on the straw bed by the wall, covered with a hairy blanket and sheepskins. The eye is now inside him, his gaze is sharp, objects look clear in the light of the oil lamp, but they are rounded at the corners. Even her face is slightly elongated in the middle and shortened at the sides in the eyes of the stout man. Through this look she is a warm young animal on the straw, in the smell of sheepskins, animal shit, sheep, silently pressing against each other, and slowly moving behind the low fence. A heavy hand reaches for her hair, but her head shakes.

"Not now," she says.

Heavy blood is crashing against the walls of his head, his ears are ringing with effort, restraint.

"Why does he call me Cretin?" he says. Anica turns her head towards him.

"Oh," she says, "that's how they registered it, for the soldiers. You should be happy," she says.

He is silent for a long time; he can smell her skin, which he can distinctly discern in the stable. He reaches for his forehead with his hand, and thinks with effort for a long time.

"Nobody will come up here for at least twenty days," he suddenly says.

Anica lowers her head. "So what? It's like this every winter."

He raises the oil lamp to her face, which looks up with its vacant eyes. Now, now suddenly something moves on it. Her face becomes even more elongated. An instant decision emerges in him, the look shakes, the animals behind the fence start pacing restlessly.

"How much longer?" he says. "How long?"

Anica moves to the wall; he turns round and pulls her towards him with a strong grip, reaches under her skirt, clawingly gathers soft matter in his fat fingers.

"He'll wake up one day," he says.

"He won't," says Anica. "I put leeches on his skin."

Now he gets up and rushes around the room so that his field of vision totters in every direction. He walks among the sheep which quietly step aside in terror; he grinds his teeth, goes back to the bed, leans close to her face.

"Put on more," he breathes into her. She shakes her head. "Put on more leeches, more."

He is breathing heavily, as after a great effort. He lies on the bed and gathers a pile of straw under his head. The wind roars along the steady slope over the ridge of the hill. The eye wants to see differently; it shifts away, rapidly moves around the room, viewing angles changing. Anica slowly gets up and puts on her fur. She takes the oil lamp and with difficulty pushes open the door, pressed back by the windy mass of the air outside. Her legs sink knee-deep into the snow; she is walking slowly, holding the lamp under the fur. The restless eye follows her; in its view the nearby landscape becomes concave at the edges; it follows her to the door and into the hall. The wind sweeps a cloud of snow inside. With a steady hand Anica takes from the shelf the black vessel with swarming little animals. The house is dark, the old man is breathing feebly, gently groaning in his dreams, his strength withering, his blood flowing away. Anica places the lamp on the chair by the bed, then she thinks of something, turns towards the room and overturns the water pot she left on the floor. The old man shifts in his sleep, the soul of a sleeping man, the soul of a sleeping man. Anica takes the crucifix off the wall, takes it into another room and covers it with her fur. She quickly returns and slips on the wet floor, stumbles towards the bed, for a moment looks at the wrinkle where the old man's eyes should be, the eyes of her aged husband, the eyes which met her, when she was fifteen years old, in front of her home and took her to this mountainous solitude; for a brief moment she looks at the sunken, tightly pressed wrinkle, then with rapid, precise movements starts placing black animals all over his body; she waits until they are stuck to his chest, bony arms, forehead and lips. The lost look of the dark angel is wildly rushing around the room, sees everything, knows everything, feels everything, all the three looks it has assumed, all the three souls, all the three bodies, the entire space for which he was bound, where he was summoned from afar. It can see and feel the old man's troubled breathing; his eyes open and look with surprise into the passing time through a blood-red veil and then blink in the coming sleep, deeper and deeper; her feverish body, the painful emptiness in her head and flesh, and the heavy, swollen male body, tossing and turning in the stable, bumping into the walls, walking among the confused and warm animals, getting up, lying down, looking with surprise at the objects around him, which are no longer only elongated in the middle and rounded at the edges, but twisted, wrapped into the spinning circle. Anica stretches herself, lets her arms droop down. She is standing, looking at the wall and in the dying light listening to the fading breathing. The wind, roaring far down in the valley. The man in the stable lies down and pulls the fur over his head. The eye moves to the corner, to the place where the crucifix used to be. It is still for some time, watching the motionless space around it. Then its look slowly moves to the door and out, into the stormy winter night. Through the white veil of the whirling snow it is moving towards the edge of the forest. There it stops and once more looks at the house at the end of the clearing, covered in snow, pressed against the slope of the large hill. Among the tree trunks, where it is almost quiet and only a little wind is slowly sinking into the forest, it swiftly moves up one of the trees, through the dark crown, and it looks over the tops of the pines bending in the wind. It roars like the sea, and its roaring descends in waves down the slope of the hill into the valley. The invisible wave blares, as if crashing against an invisible barrier. The look rests for another moment in the dark above the Pohorje forest, above Sveti Lovrenc, where the glittering eye of God is locked in the cold and empty church. The moaning of wood tissue, clawlike clutching of the roots, whirling cloud of snow being carried high up. Another look at both wooden buildings far below. Then it quickly descends with the wave, along the ridge, down into the valley.

Translated by Lili Potpara

NENAD VELIČKOVIĆ
Lodgers

Lodgers is a hilarious, unsentimental report
from the front lines of the Balkan wars of the
1990s. All of the folly and the horror of that
time are revealed in the sarcastic report of
the novel's teenage would-be authoress.

Maja lives in the basement of a Sarajevo
museum, enduring with equal annoyance
Serb artillery and vegetarian meals that taste
like fried sponge. Her father, the museum
director, zealously guards the treasures
upstairs while their aged co-lodger Julio plots
to trade them away. Maja's mother copes
with yoga while dour stepbrother Davor
endures the endless crying and cravings of his
pregnant wife. Floating amidst it all is Maja's grandmother, blind and
deaf, yet drawn to any conversation involving food.

Need and crisis propel Maja and her companions from one humorous situation to another. Yet her pitch-perfect gallows humour makes it
clear that the brutalities of war penetrate these small moments of life –
and even the self-centredness of a teenaged girl.

Nenad Veličković was born in Sarajevo in 1962. He is the author of
novels, short stories, essays, tv and radio scripts and plays. He has
received many awards for his writing and he teaches Literature at the
University of Sarajevo. He served for four years in the BiH Army and in
the early 1990s was Secretary of the Institute for Literature in Sarajevo.

ISBN 0 86322 348 6; paperback original

DAVID FOSTER
The Land Where Stories End

"Australia's most original and important living novelist." *Independent Monthly*

"A post-modern fable set in the dark ages of Ireland. . . [A] beautifully written humorous myth that is entirely original. The simplicity of language is perfectly complementary to the wry, occasionally laugh-out-loud humour and the captivating tale." *Irish World*

"I was taken by surprise and carried easily along by the amazing story and by the punchy clarity of the writing. . . This book is imaginative and fantastic. . . It is truly amazing." *Books Ireland*

ISBN 0 86322 311 7; hardback

CHET RAYMO
Valentine

"Such nebulous accounts [as we have] have been just waiting for someone to make a work of historical fiction out of them. American novelist and physicist Raymo has duly obliged with his recently published *Valentine: A Love Story*." *The Scotsman*

"[A] vivid and lively account of how Valentine's life may have unfolded... Raymo has produced an imaginative and enjoyable read, sprinkled with plenty of food for philosophical thought." *Sunday Tribune*

ISBN 0 86322 327 3; paperback original

PJ CURTIS
The Lightning Tree

This unique novel tells the story of Mariah, a woman healer who lived in harmony not only with the special environment of the Burren but with the spirits of past generations; a woman who drank deep from the well of traditional wisdom, yet whose view of the world resonates with meaning for the present and future.

"Mariah's voice comes from an Ireland in which there was time and space to attend to the delicate details of both the natural and the supernatural worlds. In PJ Curtis's hands, her story becomes a poignant elegy for that more beautiful Ireland." Nuala O'Faolain

ISBN 0 86322 347 8; paperback original

BRYAN MACMAHON
Hero Town

"*Hero Town* is the perfect retrospective: here the town is the hero, a character of epic and comic proportions. . . It may come to be recognized as MacMahon's masterpiece." Professor Bernard O'Donohue

"For the course of a calendar year, Peter Mulrooney, the musing pedagogue, saunters through the streets and the people, looking at things and leaving them so. They talk to him; he listens, and in his ears we hear the authentic voice of local Ireland, all its tics and phrases and catchcalls. Like Joyce, this wonderful, excellently structured book comes alive when you read it aloud." Frank Delaney, *Sunday Independent*

ISBN 0 86322 342 7; paperback

KEN BRUEN

"Outstanding. . . . Ireland's version of Scotland's Ian Rankin."
Publishers Weekly

"Exhibits Ken Bruen's all-encompassing ability to depict the underbelly of the criminal world and still imbue it with a torrid fascination... carrying an adrenalin charge for those who like their thrillers rough, tough, mean and dirty." *The Irish Times*

ISBN 0 86322 302 8; paperback

"Collectively, the Jack Taylor novels are Bruen's masterwork, and *The Dramatist* is the darkest and most profound installment of the series to date. A clean and sober Taylor – a man who has always been a danger to his friends – proves infinitely more destructive to those around him. The senseless death of a recurring character brings *The Dramatist* to a crushing conclusion. The novel's chilling final image of Taylor could serve as a dictionary illustration for noir. Readers who dare the journey will be days shaking this most haunting book out of their heads." *This Week*

ISBN 0 86322 319 2; paperback original

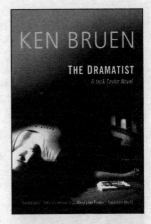

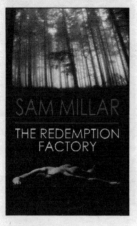

SAM MILLAR
The Redemption Factory

"He writes well, with a certain raw energy, and he is not afraid to take risks with his fiction. The result is a novel that can sometimes be as shocking as it is original." *Irish Independent*

A man is murdered, an anarchist suspected by his own group of being a police informer, but the killer has his doubts. Years later, in a deserted wood a corrupt businessman, Shank, silences a whistleblower. Lurking sometimes at the edge of the action, sometimes at the centre, is the deeply dysfunctional family of Shank and his two strange daughters, and their gruesome abattoir.

ISBN 0 86322 339 7; paperback original

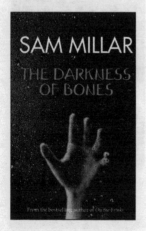

SAM MILLAR
The Darkness of Bones

A tense tale of murder, betrayal, sexual abuse and revenge, and the corruption at the heart of the respectable establishment

A young boy discovers a bone in a snow-covered forest. Initially, he thinks it could simply be that of an animal. But it belongs to a young girl who has been missing for three years. Meanwhile, in a derelict orphanage, a tramp discovers the sexually mutilated and decapitated corpse of its former head warden.

ISBN 0 86322 350 8; paperback original

JACK BARRY
Miss Katie Regrets

From the criminal underbelly of Celtic Tiger
Dublin comes a gripping story of guns, drugs,
prostitution and corruption.

A seemingly humdrum shooting leads a
detective to an online male prostitution service
and to hints of a link with a corrupt politician.

The plot moves between Dublin and
Amsterdam, Manchester and British suburbia.
At the centre of an apparent spider's web of
intrigue sits the enigmatic figure of Miss Katie,
a crabby Dublin transvestite who will, under
pressure, kiss and tell. And, perhaps, kill.

ISBN 0 86322 354 0; paperback original

KEN BRUEN (ED)
Dublin Noir

Nineteen previously unpublished stories by
acclaimed crime writers, each one set in
Dublin

Brand new stories by Ray Banks, James O.
Born, Ken Bruen, Reed Farrell Coleman, Eoin
Colfer, Jim Fusilli, Patrick J. Lambe, Laura
Lippman, Craig McDonald, Pat Mullan, Gary
Phillips, John Rickards, Peter Spiegelman,
Jason Starr, Olen Steinhauer, Charlie Stella,
Duane Swierczynski, Sarah Weinman and
Kevin Wignall.

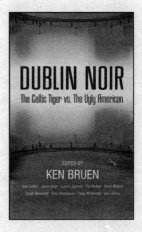

ISBN 0 86322 353 2; paperback original

KITTY FITZGERALD
Small Acts of Treachery

"Mystery and politics, a forbidden sexual attraction that turns into romance; Kitty Fitzgerald takes the reader on a gripping roller coaster through the recent past. In *Small Acts of Treachery* a woman of courage defies the power not only of the secret state but of sinister global elites. This is a story you can't stop reading, with an undertow which will give you cause to reflect." Sheila Rowbotham

"[It] is a super book with a fascinating story and great characters . . . all the more impressive because of the very sinister feeling I was left with that it is all too frighteningly possible." *Books Ireland*

ISBN 086322 297 8; paperback

KATE McCAFFERTY
Testimony of an Irish Slave Girl

"McCafferty's haunting novel chronicles an overlooked chapter in the annals of human slavery . . . A meticulously researched piece of historical fiction that will keep readers both horrified and mesmerized." *Booklist*

"Thousands of Irish men, women and children were sold into slavery to work in the sugar-cane fields of Barbados in the 17th century . . . McCafferty has researched her theme well and, through Cot, shows us the terrible indignities and suffering endured." *Irish Independent*

ISBN 0 86322 314 1; hardback
ISBN 0 86322 338 9; paperback